Old Masters

Thomas Bernhard was born in 1931 in Heerlen, the Netherlands and grew up in Salzburg and Vienna. He trained to be an actor and singer, but persistent ill health made these careers impossible. Starting with *Gargoyles* in 1967 he began, through a series of novels and plays, his devastating assault on the 'mindless cultural sewer' of Austria. Gleefully setting out to be as offensive as possible, Bernhard wrote his major works, including the play *Heldenplatz* and the novels *Cutting Timber*, *Old Masters* and *Extinction* and the micro-stories *The Voice Imitator*. He died in Gmunden, Upper Austria in 1989, forbidding in his will any further publication or performance of his work in Austria.

THOMAS BERNHARD

Old Masters

A Comedy

Translated from the German by Ewald Osers

PENGUIN BOOKS

PENGUIN CLASSICS

Published by the Penguin Group
Penguin Books Ltd, 80 Strand, London WC2R ORL, England
Penguin Group (USA), Inc., 375 Hudson Street, New York, New York 10014, USA
Penguin Group (Canada), 90 Eglinton Avenue East, Suite 700, Toronto, Ontario, Canada M4P 2Y3
(a division of Pearson Penguin Canada Inc.)
Penguin Ireland, 25 St Stephen's Green, Dublin 2, Ireland (a division of Penguin Books Ltd)
Penguin Group (Australia), 250 Camberwell Road, Camberwell, Victoria 3124, Australia
(a division of Pearson Australia Group Pty Ltd)
Penguin Books India Pvt Ltd, 11 Community Centre, Panchsheel Park, New Delhi – 110 017, India
Penguin Group (NZ), 67 Apollo Drive, Rosedale, North Shore 0632, New Zealand
(a division of Pearson New Zealand Ltd)
Penguin Books (South Africa) (Pty) Ltd, 24 Sturdee Avenue, Rosebank, Johannesburg 2196, South Africa

Penguin Books Ltd, Registered Offices: 80 Strand, London WC2R ORL, England

www.penguin.com

First published as *Alte Meister* by Suhrkamp Verlag 1985
This edition originally published by the University of Chicago Press in arrangement with Quartet
Books 1989
Published in Penguin Classics 2010

002

Translation copyright © Ewald Osers, 1989
All rights reserved

The moral right of the translator has been asserted

Set in 13/15.25 pt Dante MT
Typeset by Ellipsis Books Limited, Glasgow
Printed in England by Clays Ltd, St Ives plc

978 – 0 – 141 – 19271 – 0

www.greenpenguin.co.uk

The punishment matches the guilt: to be deprived of all appetite for life, to be brought to the highest degree of weariness of life

Kierkegaard

Although I had arranged to meet Reger at the *Kunsthistorisches Museum* at half-past eleven, I arrived at the agreed spot at half-past ten in order, as I had for some time decided to do, to observe him, for once, from the most ideal angle possible and undisturbed, Atzbacher writes. As he had his morning spot in the so-called Bordone Room, facing Tintoretto's *White-Bearded Man*, on the velvet-covered settee on which yesterday, after an explanation of the so-called *Tempest Sonata*, he continued his lecture to me on the *Art of the Fugue*, from *before* Bach to *after* Schumann, as he put it, and yet was in the mood to talk rather more about Mozart and not about Bach, I had to take up position in the so-called Sebastiano Room; I was compelled therefore, entirely against my inclination, to submit to Titian in order to be able to observe Reger in front of Tintoretto's *White-Bearded Man*, moreover standing, which was no disadvantage because

I

I prefer standing to sitting, especially when engaged in observing people, and I have all my life been a better observer standing up than sitting down, and as, looking from the Sebastiano Room into the Bordone Room, I eventually, by focusing as hard as I could, was able to see Reger completely in profile, not even impaired by the back-rest of the settee, Reger who, no doubt badly affected by the sudden change in the weather during the preceding night, kept his black hat on his head the whole time, so as I was therefore able to see the whole left side of Reger exposed to me, my plan to observe Reger undisturbed for once had succeeded. As Reger (in an overcoat), supporting himself on a stick wedged between his knees, was totally absorbed in viewing the *White-Bearded Man* I had not the least fear, while observing Reger, of being discovered by him. The attendant Irrsigler (Jenö!), with whom Reger is linked by an acquaintanceship of more than thirty years and with whom I myself have always to this day had good relations (also for over twenty years), had been warned by a hand signal on my part that for once I wished to observe Reger undisturbed, and whenever Irrsigler appeared, with clockwork regularity, he acted as if I were not there at all, just as he acted as if Reger were not there at all, while he, Irrsigler, discharging his duty, subjected the visitors to the gallery, who, incomprehensibly on this free-admission Saturday, were not numerous, to his customary (for anyone who did not know him) disagreeable scrutiny. Irrsigler has that irritating stare which museum attendants employ in order to intimidate the visitors who, as is well known, are endowed with all kinds of bad behaviour; his manner of abruptly and utterly soundlessly appearing round the corner of whatever room in order to inspect it is indeed repulsive to anyone who does not know him; in his grey uniform, badly cut and yet intended for eternity, held together by large black buttons and hanging on his meagre body as if from a coat rack, and with his peaked cap tailored from the same grey cloth, he is more reminiscent of a warder in one of our penal institutions than of a state-employed guardian of works of art. Ever since I have known him Irrsigler has always been as pale as he now is, even though he is not sick, and Reger has for decades described him as *a state corpse on duty at the Kunsthistorisches Museum for over thirty-six years*. Reger, who has been coming to the Kunsthistorisches Museum for over thirty-six years, has known Irrsigler from the first day of his employment and maintains an entirely amicable relationship with him. *It only required a very small bribe to secure the settee in the Bordone Room forever*, Reger told me some years ago. Reger entered into a relationship with Irrsigler which has become a habit for both of them for over thirty years. Whenever Reger, as happens not infrequently, wishes to be alone in his contemplation of Tintoretto's *White-Bearded Man*, Irrsigler quite simply blocks the Bordone Room to visitors, he quite simply places himself in the doorway and lets no one pass. Reger need only give a hand signal and Irrsigler blocks the Bordone Room, indeed he does not shrink from pushing any visitors already in the Bordone Room out of the Bordone Room, because that is Reger's wish. Irrsigler finished an apprenticeship as a carpenter in Bruck-on-Leitha but gave up carpentry even *before* qualifying as an assistant carpenter in order to become a policeman. The police, however, turned Irrsigler down because of his *physical weakness*. An uncle, a brother of his mother, who had been an attendant at the Kunsthistorisches Museum since nineteen twenty-four, got him his post at the Kunsthistorisches Museum, *the most underpaid but the most secure*, as Irrsigler says. Anyway, Irrsigler had only wanted to join the police because the career of a policeman would, as he believed, solve his clothing problem. To slip all one's life into the same clothes without even having to pay for those clothes out of his own pocket because the state provided them, appeared to him ideal, and his uncle, who got him into the Kunsthistorisches Museum, had thought the same way, and anyway there was no difference in this respect between being employed by the police and being employed by the Kunsthistorisches Museum, admittedly the police paid more and the Kunsthistorisches Museum less, but then service in the Kunsthistorisches Museum could not be compared with service in the police, he, Irrsigler, could not imagine a *more responsible but at the same time easier service* than in the Kunsthistorisches Museum. In the police, Irrsigler said, a man served day after day in danger of his life; not so if he served at the Kunsthistorisches Museum. As for the monotony of his occupation there was no need to worry, he loved that monotony. Each day he would cover some forty to fifty kilometres, which was more beneficial to his health than, for instance, service in the police, where the main part of the job was sitting on a hard office chair, life-long. He would *rather shadow visitors to the museum than normal people*, for visitors to the museum were at any rate *superior people with an understanding of art*. In the course of time he had, he said, acquired such an understanding of art that he would be capable at any time of guiding a conducted tour through the Kunsthistorisches Museum, or certainly through the picture gallery, but he could do without that. Anyway, people do not take in what is said to them, he says. *For decades the museum guides have always been saying the same thing, and of course a great deal of nonsense, as*

Herr Reger says, Irrsigler says to me. *The art historians only swamp the visitors with their twaddle*, says Irrsigler, who has, over the years, appropriated verbatim many, if not all, of Reger's sentences. Irrsigler is Reger's mouthpiece, nearly everything that Irrsigler says has been said by Reger, for over thirty years Irrsigler has been saying what Reger has said. If I listen attentively I can hear Reger speak through Irrsigler. *If we listen to the guides we only ever hear that art twaddle which gets on our nerves, the unbearable art twaddle of the art historians*, says Irrsigler, because Reger says so frequently. *All these paintings are magnificent, but not a single one is perfect*, Irrsigler says after Reger. People only go to the museum because they have been told that a cultured person must go there, and not out of interest, people are not interested in art, at any rate ninety-nine per cent of humanity has no interest whatever in art, as Irrsigler says, quoting Reger word for word. He, Irrsigler, had had a difficult childhood, a mother suffering from cancer and dying when she was only forty-six, and a womanizing and perpetually drunk father. And *Bruck-on-Leitha, moreover, is such an ugly place, as are most of the places in Burgenland.* Anyone who can do so leaves the Burgenland, Irrsigler says, but most of them cannot, they are sentenced to Burgenland for life, which is at least as terrible as imprisonment for life at Stein-on-Danube. The

Burgenlanders are convicts, says Irrsigler, their native land is a penal institution. They try to make themselves believe that they have a beautiful homeland, but in reality Burgenland is boring and ugly. In winter the Burgenlanders choke in snow and in summer they are eaten alive by mosquitoes. And in spring and autumn the Burgenlanders only wallow in their own filth. In the whole of Europe there is no poorer and no filthier region, Irrsigler says. The Viennese are forever persuading the Burgenlanders that Burgenland is a beautiful province, because the Viennese are in love with Burgenland filth and with Burgenland dim-wittedness because they regard this Burgenland filth and this Burgenland dim-wittedness *as romantic*, because in their Viennese way they are perverse. Anyway, *apart from Herr Haydn, as Herr Reger says*, Burgenland has produced nothing, Irrsigler says. I come from Burgenland means nothing other than I come from Austria's penal institution. Or from Austria's mental institution, Irrsigler says. *The Burgenlanders go to Vienna as if to church*, he says. A Burgenlander's fondest wish is to join the Vienna police, he said a few days ago, I failed to do so because I was too weak, because of *physical weakness*. Anyway I am an attendant at the Kunsthistorisches Museum and just as much a public servant. In the evening, after six, I do not lock up any criminals but works of art, I lock up Rubens and Bellotto. His uncle, who had entered the services of the Kunsthistorisches Museum immediately after the First World War, had been envied by everyone in the family. Whenever they had visited him at the Kunsthistorisches Museum, once in every few years, on free-admission Saturdays or Sundays, they had always followed him *totally intimidated through the rooms with the great masters* and had not ceased to admire *his uniform*. Naturally his uncle had soon become Senior Attendant and had worn a small brass star on his uniform lapel, Irrsigler said. With all that reverence and admiration they had, as he was leading them through the rooms, understood nothing of what he said to them. There would have been no point in explaining Veronese to them, Irrsigler said a few days ago. My sister's children, Irrsigler said, admired my soft shoes, my sister stopped in front of the Reni, in front of that most tasteless of all painters exhibited here. Reger hates Reni, therefore Irrsigler hates Reni too. Irrsigler has achieved a high degree of mastery in appropriating Reger's statements, indeed he now utters them almost perfectly in Reger's characteristic tone. My sister visits *me and not the museum*, Irrsigler said. My sister does not care for art at all. But her children are amazed at everything they see when I guide them through the rooms. They stop in front of the Velazquez and refuse to move away from it, Irrsigler said. Herr Reger once invited me and my family to the Prater, Irrsigler said, *the generous Herr Reger, on a Sunday evening. When his wife was still alive*, Irrsigler said. I stood there, watching Reger, who was still *engrossed*, as they say, in contemplating Tintoretto's *White-Bearded Man*, and simultaneously saw Irrsigler, who was not in the Bordone Room, recounting to me chunks of his life story, i.e. the images with Irrsigler from the past week at the same time as Reger, who was sitting on the velvet settee, and naturally, had not yet noticed me. Irrsigler had said that even as a small child his fondest wish had been to join the Vienna police, to be a policeman. He had never wanted to have any other profession. And when, at the time he was twenty-three, they had confirmed *physical weakness* in him at the Rossau barracks, a *world had collapsed for* him. In his state of extreme hopelessness, however, his uncle had got him an attendant's position at the Kunsthistorisches Museum. He had come to Vienna with nothing but a small scuffed portmanteau, to his uncle's flat, who had let him stay with him for four weeks, after which he, Irrsigler, had moved as a lodger to the Mölkerbastei. In that rented room he had lived for twelve years. During those first few years he had seen nothing of Vienna at all, he had gone to the Kunsthistorisches Museum in the early morning, towards seven, and had returned home in the evening, after six, his midday meal all those years had invariably consisted of a slice of bread with salami or with cheese, consumed with a glass of water from the tap in a small dressing room behind the public cloakroom. Burgenlanders are the most undemanding of people, I have myself worked with Burgenlanders at various building sites in my youth and lived with Burgenlanders in various builders' hutments, and I know how undemanding these Burgenlanders are, they only need the most indispensable things and actually manage to save some eighty per cent or even more of their wages by the end of the month. As I was scrutinizing Irrsigler and actually observing him intently, as I had never observed him before, I could see Irrsigler standing with me in the Battoni Room the previous week and me listening to him. The husband of one of his great-grandmothers had come from the Tyrol, hence the name Irrsigler. He had had two sisters, the younger one, as late as the sixties, had emigrated to America with a hairdresser's assistant from Mattersburg and had died there of homesickness, at the age of thirty-five. He had three brothers, all of them living in Burgenland as casual labourers. Two of them, like himself, had come to Vienna to join the police but had not been accepted. And for the museum service, he said, *a certain intelligence was absolutely necessary.*

He had learned a lot from Reger. There were people who said Reger was mad because only a madman could for decades go every other day except Monday to the picture gallery of the Kunsthistorisches Museum, but he did not believe that. *Herr Reger is a clever, educated man*, Irrsigler said. Yes, I had said to Irrsigler, Herr Reger is not only a clever and educated man, but also a famous man, after all he had studied music in Leipzig and Vienna and written music reviews for *The Times* and was writing for *The Times* to this day, I said. Not an ordinary scribbler, I said, not a chatterbox, but a musical scholar in the truest sense of the word and with the full seriousness of a great personality. Reger was not to be compared with all those garrulous musical columnists, who poured out their garrulous refuse in the daily papers day after day. Reger was in fact a philosopher, I said to Irrsigler, a philosopher in the full clear meaning of the term. For over thirty years Reger has written his reviews for *The Times*, those little musical-philosophical essays which would no doubt one day be brought together and appear in book form. This sojourn in the Kunsthistorisches Museum is undoubtedly one of the prerequisites of Reger's being able to write for *The Times in just the way* he does write for *The Times*, I said to Irrsigler; regardless of whether or not Irrsigler understood me, probably Irrsigler did not understand me at all, I thought and still think. That Reger writes his musical criticism for *The Times* is not known to anyone in Austria, or at most a few people know about it, I said to Irrsigler. I might also say *Reger is a private philosopher*, I said to Irrsigler, regardless of the fact that it was rather a stupid thing to say to Irrsigler. At the Kunsthistorisches Museum Reger finds what he does not find anywhere else, I said to Irrsigler, everything that is important, everything that is useful to his thinking and to his work. People may regard Reger's behaviour as mad, which it is not, I said to Irrsigler, here in Vienna and in Austria Reger is not taken note of, I said to Irrsigler, but in London and England, and even in the United States, people know who Reger is and what an outstanding expert Reger is, I said to Irrsigler. And do not forget the ideal temperature of eighteen degrees Celsius, which is maintained here all the year round at the Kunsthistorisches Museum, I also said to Irrsigler. Irrsigler only nodded his head. Reger is a figure highly thought of throughout the world of musical scholarship, I said to Irrsigler yesterday, only here, in his native country, no one wants to know about him, on the contrary, here in his native country, Reger, who has left all the others in his field far behind him, that whole revolting provincial incompetence, is being hated, yes, nothing less than hated in his native Austria, I said to Irrsigler.

A genius like Reger is hated here, I said to Irrsigler, regardless of the fact that Irrsigler had not understood at all what I meant by saying to him that a genius like Reger was hated here, and regardless of whether it is actually correct to speak of Reger as of a genius, *a scholarly genius, and indeed a human genius*, I reflected, that Reger was certainly. Genius and Austria do not go together, I said. In Austria one has to be mediocre in order to be listened to and taken seriously, one has to be a person of incompetence and of provincial mendacity, a person with an absolute small-country mentality. A genius or even an exceptional mind is sooner or later *finished off* here in a humiliating manner, I said to Irrsigler. Only people like Reger, whom one can count on the fingers of one hand in this dreadful country, survive this state of degradation and hatred, of oppression and disregard, of that universal anti-intellectual meanness which reigns everywhere in Austria, only people with a magnificent character and a truly acute incorruptible intelligence. Although Herr Reger has a far from unhappy relationship with the directress of this museum and although he knows this directress well, I said to Irrsigler, he would never have dreamt of asking this directress for anything concerning himself and this museum. Just as Herr Reger had decided he would inform the management, and that means the directress, of the shabby state of the settee covers in the rooms and possibly induce her to have new settee covers made, the settees were re-covered; and very tastefully too, I said to Irrsigler. I do not believe, I said to Irrsigler, that the management of the Kunsthistorisches Museum is aware that Herr Reger has been coming to the museum every other day for more than thirty years in order to sit on the settee in the Bordone Room, that I do not believe. Because that would surely have cropped up in conversation at a meeting between Reger and the directress, as far as I know, the directress is unaware of it because Herr Reger never mentioned it and because you, Herr Irrsigler, have always kept quiet about it because it has been Herr Reger's wish that you would keep quiet about the fact that for over thirty years Herr Reger has been visiting the Kunsthistorisches Museum every other day except Mondays. Discretion, that is your very strong suit, I said to Irrsigler, I reflected, while regarding Reger who was in turn regarding Tintoretto's *White-Bearded Man* and who, for his part, was being regarded by Irrsigler. Reger was an exceptional person and exceptional persons had to be handled carefully, I said to Irrsigler yesterday. That we, that is Reger and I, should visit the museum on two successive days is unthinkable, I said to Irrsigler yesterday, and yet I have come back today, of all days, because Reger had expressly wished me to do so, but for what reason

Reger is here today I do not know, I reflected, but I should soon know it. Irrsigler, too, had been rather astonished when he saw me today, because only yesterday I had told him that it was quite out of the question that I should go to the Kunsthistorisches Museum two days running, just as until now it had been out of the question for Reger. And now we are both, Reger and myself, back today at the Kunsthistorisches Museum, where we were only yesterday. This must have confused Irrsigler, I thought. It was possible, I thought, to make a mistake for once and therefore go to the Kunsthistorisches Museum again the next day, but surely, I reflected, only for *Reger alone* to make such a mistake or for *me alone* to make such a mistake, but surely not for *both of us, Reger and me*, to make a mistake on this point. Reger had expressly said to me yesterday, *Come here tomorrow*, I can still hear Reger saying it. But Irrsigler, of course, had not heard anything about it and did not know anything about it and was, quite naturally, astonished to see Reger and me back at the museum today. If Reger had not said to me yesterday: Come here tomorrow, I should not have come to the Kunsthistorisches Museum today, possibly not until next week, for unlike Reger, who in fact goes to the Kunsthistorisches Museum every other day, and has moreover done so for decades, I do not go to the Kunsthistorisches Museum every other day but only when I feel like it and when I am in the mood for it. And if I wish to see Reger I do not necessarily have to go to the Kunsthistorisches Museum, I only have to go to the *Ambassador* Hotel, where he always goes after leaving the Kunsthistorisches Museum. At the Ambassador I can see Reger every day if I am so disposed. At the Ambassador he has his corner by the window, that is the table next to the so-called *Jewish table*, which stands in front of the *Hungarian table*, which stands behind the *Arab table* when you look from Reger's table towards the door to the foyer. Of course I much prefer going to the Ambassador rather than to the Kunsthistorisches Museum, but when I cannot wait for Reger to come to the Ambassador I go to the Kunsthistorisches Museum a little before eleven in order to meet him, my imaginary father. Until noon he finds the eighteen-degree temperature at the Kunsthistorisches Museum agreeable, in the afternoon he is happier at the warm Ambassador, which always keeps a temperature of twenty-three degrees. In the afternoon I am no longer so fond of thinking nor do I think so intensively, Reger says, so I can afford the Ambassador. The Kunsthistorisches Museum is his *mental production shop*, he says, while the Ambassador is, in a manner of speaking, his *ideas-processing machine*. At the Kunsthistorisches Museum I feel exposed, at the Ambassador I feel sheltered, he says. This contrast of Kunsthistorisches Museum and Ambassador is what my thinking needs more than anything else, exposure on the one side and shelter on the other, the atmosphere at the Kunsthistorisches Museum on the one side and the atmosphere at the Ambassador on the other, exposure on the one side and shelter on the other, my dear Atzbacher; the secret of my thinking is based on my spending the morning at the Kunsthistorisches Museum and the afternoon at the Ambassador. And what greater opposites could there be than the Kunsthistorisches Museum, that is the picture gallery of the Kunsthistorisches Museum, and the Ambassador. I have made the Kunsthistorisches Museum a mental habit for myself just as the Ambassador, he said. The quality of my reviews for *The Times*, to which, incidentally, I have been a contributor for thirty-four years, he said, in fact depends on my visiting the Kunsthistorisches Museum and the Ambassador, the Kunsthistorisches Museum *every other* morning, the Ambassador *every* afternoon. This routine alone saved me after the death of my wife. My dear Atzbacher, without this routine I should have died too, Reger said yesterday. Everybody needs such a routine for survival, he said. It may be the craziest of all routines but he needs it. Reger's condition seems to have improved, his way of speaking is once more the same as before the death of his wife. Although he says he has now got over the *dead point*, he will neverthe-less suffer all his life from having been left on his own by his wife. Time and again he says that he had been trapped in the lifelong mistaken belief that *he* would leave his wife, that *he* would die before her, and because her death came so suddenly he had been firmly convinced, even a few days before her death, that *she* was going to survive him; *she* was the healthy one, *I* was the invalid, yes, it was in this belief and in this conviction that we always lived, he said. Nobody has ever been so healthy as my wife, *she lived a whole life in health, whereas I have always led an existence in sickness, indeed an existence in mortal sickness*, he said. She was the healthy one, she was the future, I was always the invalid, I was the past, he said. That he would ever have to live without his wife and actually on his own had never occurred to him, that was no thought for me, he said. And if she should die before me I would follow her into death, as quickly as possible, he had always thought. Now he had come to grips, on the one hand, with the error that she would die after him and, on the other, with the fact that he had not killed himself after her death, that he had not therefore, as he had intended, followed her into death. As I always knew that she was everything to me I was naturally unable to think of continued existence after her, my dear Atzbacher, he said. Out of this human weakness, though in fact it is unworthy of a human being, out of this cowardice, I did not follow her into death, but on the contrary, as it seems to me now (as he said yesterday), I have grown stronger, at times I have recently felt that I am stronger than ever. I now cling to life even more than in the past, whether you believe it or not, I am in fact holding on to life with the wildest fervour. I do not want to admit it, but I live with an even greater intensity than before her death. True, it took me over a year even to be able to think this thought, but now I am thinking this thought, without embarrassment, he said. What depresses me so excessively is the fact that such a receptive person as my wife was should die *with all that enormous knowledge which I conveyed to her,* that she should have taken that enormous knowledge into death with her, that is the worst enormity, an enormity far worse than the fact that she is dead, he said. We force and we stuff everything within us into such a person, and then that person leaves us, dies on us, forever, he said. Added to it is *the suddenness* of it, the fact that we did not foresee the death of that person, not for one moment did I foresee the death of my wife, I looked upon her just as if she had eternal life, never thought of her death, he said, just as if she really lived *with my knowledge right into infinity as an infinity,* he said. Really a precipitate death, he said. We take such a person for eternity, that is the mistake. Had I known she was going to die on me I should have acted entirely differently, as it was I did not know she was going to die on me and before me and so I acted utterly senselessly, just as though she existed infinitely into infinity, whereas she was not made for infinity at all but for finiteness, like all of us. Only if we love a person with such unbridled love as I loved my wife do we in fact believe that person will live forever and into infinity. Never before, when sitting on the settee in that Bordone Room, had he kept his hat on, and just as the fact that he had ordered me to the museum for today disquieted me, because this was really the most unusual fact imaginable, as I thought, the fact that he had kept his hat on while sitting on the settee in the Bordone Room was most unusual, quite apart from a whole string of other unusual circumstances in this connection. Irrsigler had stepped into the Bordone Room and, having walked over to him, whispered something into Reger's ear, only to leave the Bordone Room immediately afterwards. Irrsigler's communication, however, at least viewed from the outside, produced no effect on Reger, after Irrsigler's communication Reger remained sitting on the settee just as before Irrsigler's communication. Nevertheless I was reflecting on what Irrsigler might have said to Reger. But I immediately gave up my reflections on what Irrsigler might have said to Reger and instead observed Reger and simultaneously heard him saying to me: People go to the Kunsthistorisches Museum because it is the done thing, they even travel to Vienna from Spain and Portugal and go to the Kunsthistorisches Museum so that back home in Spain and Portugal they can say that they have been to the Kunsthistorisches Museum in Vienna, which is surely ridiculous as the Kunsthistorisches Museum is not the Prado, nor the Lisbon Museum, the Kunsthistorisches Museum is a long way from being that. The Kunsthistorisches Museum does not even have a Goya and it does not even have an El Greco. I saw Reger and observed him and simultaneously heard what he had said to me the day before. *The Kunsthistorisches Museum does not even have a Goya, it does not even have an El Greco.* Of course it can do without the El Greco, because El Greco is not a really great, not a first-class painter, Reger said, but not to have a Goya is downright fatal for a museum such as the Kunsthistorisches Museum. No Goya, he said, that is just like the Habsburgs who, as you know, had no understanding of art, an ear for music certainly, but no understanding of art. They listened to Beethoven but they did not see Goya. They did not want to have Goya. To Beethoven they accorded a fool's licence because music was not dangerous to them, but Goya was not allowed into

Austria. Well, the Habsburgs have exactly this dubious Catholic taste which is at home in this museum. The Kunsthistorisches Museum is exactly that dubious Habsburg taste in art, aesthetic and repulsive. The way we talk to people who do not concern us in the least, he said, just because we need listeners. We need listeners and a mouthpiece, he said. All our lives we wish for an ideal mouthpiece and do not find it, for there is no ideal mouthpiece. We have an Irrsigler, he said, yet we are searching all the time for an ideal Irrsigler. We make a completely simple person our mouthpiece, and when we have made that completely simple person our mouthpiece we search for another mouthpiece, for another person suitable to be our mouthpiece, he said. After the death of my wife I have at least Irrsigler, he said. Irrsigler, like all Burgen-landers, was only a Burgenlandish dim-wit before he encountered me, Reger said. We need a dim-wit for a mouthpiece. A Burgenlandish dim-wit is an entirely suitable mouthpiece, Reger said. Don't misunderstand me, I esteem Irrsigler, I need him now like a piece of bread, I have needed him for decades, but only a dim-wit like Irrsigler is usable as a mouthpiece, Reger said yesterday. Of course we exploit such a dim-wit as a human being, he said, but on the other hand, by the very fact that we exploit him, we turn *such a dim-wit into a human being*, by making him our mouthpiece and forcing our ideas into him, rather inconsiderately at first, granted, we make a Burgenlandish dim-wit, such as Irrsigler was, into a Burgenlandish human being. Before he encountered me, Irrsigler, for instance, had no notion of music, or of any of the arts, basically of nothing, not even of his dim-wittedness. Now Irrsigler is more advanced than any of those art-history twaddlers who come here day after day and assail people's ears with their art-history inanities. Irrsigler is more advanced than those art-history lecturing swine who every day with their twaddle ruin dozens of school classes, whom they drive before them, for life. The art historians are the real wreckers of art, Reger said. The art historians twaddle so long about art until they have killed it with their twaddle. Art is killed by the twaddle of the art historians. My God, I often think, sitting here on the settee while the art historians are driving their helpless flocks past me, what a pity about all these people who have all art driven out of them, driven out of them for good, by these very art historians. The art historians' trade is the vilest trade there is, and a twaddling art historian, but then there are only twaddling art historians, deserves to be chased out with a whip, chased out of the world of art, Reger said, all art historians deserve to be chased out of the world of art, because art historians are the real wreckers of art and we should not allow art to be wrecked by the art historians who are really art wreckers. Listening to an art historian we feel sick, he said, by listening to an art historian we see the art he is twaddling about being ruined, with the twaddle of the art historian art shrivels and is ruined. Thousands, indeed tens of thousands of art historians wreck art by their twaddle and ruin it, he said. The art historians are the real killers of art, if we listen to an art historian we participate in the wrecking of art, wherever an art historian appears art is wrecked, that is the truth. In all my life, therefore, I hardly ever hated anything with a fiercer hatred than art historians, Reger said. To listen to Irrsigler when he explains a painting to an innocent visitor is pure joy, Reger said, because in explaining a work of art he is never garrulous, he is not a twaddler, only a modest en-lightener and reporter who leaves the work of art open to the beholder, who does not close it for him with his twaddling. That is what I taught him, Irrsigler, over the decades, how works of art should be explained as something to be contemplated. But of course anything Irrsigler says comes from me, Reger added, because naturally he has nothing of his own, but he has the best that there is in my head, even though learned second-hand, but useful now and again. The so-called fine arts are exceedingly useful to a music-ologist like myself, Reger said, the more I concentrate on musicology and, actually, the more I have got stuck fast in musicology, the more intensively I concern myself with fine arts; conversely I think that is of the greatest advantage to, for instance, a painter if he devotes himself to music, in the sense that if he has decided on lifelong painting he should also pursue lifelong musical studies. The fine arts complement music in a wonderful way and the one is always beneficial to the other, he said. I could not imagine my musicological studies without a discussion with the so-called fine arts, especially with painting, he said. I handle my musical concerns so well because simultaneously, and with no less enthusiasm and no less intensity, I am concerned with painting. It is not for nothing that I have been going to the Kunsthistorisches Museum for over thirty years. Others go to a tavern in the morning and drink three or four glasses of beer, I sit down here and contemplate the Tintoretto. Crazy, perhaps, as you are bound to think, but I cannot do otherwise. For some it is their favourite lifelong habit to drink three or four glasses of beer at some mid-morning tavern, while I go to the Kunsthistorisches Museum. Some person may take a bath around eleven in the morning to help him clear his daily hurdle, while I go to the Kunsthistorisches Museum. If in addition we have a man like Irrsigler we have all we need, Reger said. Actually, I have never, ever since childhood, hated anything more than museums, he said, I am by nature a hater of museums, but it is probably just because of this that I have been coming here for over thirty years, I indulge in this doubtlessly mentally determined absurdity. As you know, I do not come to the Bordone Room for Bordone, indeed not even for Tintoretto, even though I consider the *White-Bearded Man* one of the most magnificent paintings ever painted, I come to the Bordone Room here for this settee and for the ideal effect which the lighting has on my emotional capacity, actually for the ideal temperature conditions especially in the Bordone Room, and for Irrsigler who is the real Irrsigler only in the Bordone Room. The truth is I could never endure being in the vicinity of, for instance, Velazquez. Not to mention Rigaud and Largilliere whom I avoid like the plague. Here in the Bordone Room I have the best conditions for meditation, and if I ever felt like reading anything on this settee, such as my beloved Montaigne or my perhaps even better loved Pascal or my even better-loved-still Voltaire, as you see my favourite authors are all French, not a single German, I can do so here in the most agreeable and the most useful way. The Bordone Room is my thinking as well as my reading room. And if I ever feel like a sip of water, Irrsigler brings me a glass, I do not even have to get up. People are sometimes surprised to

see me here, sitting on the settee, reading my Voltaire
and drinking a glass of pure water with it, they are
astonished, they shake their heads and move on, and
it is as if they regarded me as a madman enjoying a
special state-authorized fool's licence. I have not read
a book at home for years, here in the Bordone Room
I have read hundreds of books, but that is not to say
that I read all those books in the Bordone Room
through to the end, I have never in my life read a single
book *through to the end*, my way of reading a book is
that of a highly talented page turner, that is of a
person who would rather turn the pages than read,
who therefore turns dozens, or at times hundreds,
of pages before reading a single one; but when this
person does read a page he reads it more thoroughly
than anyone and with the greatest reading passion
imaginable. I am more of a page turner than a reader,
you should know, and I love turning pages just as
much as reading, I have, in my life, turned pages a
million times more often than I have read them, and
always derived from turning pages at least as much
pleasure and real intellectual enjoyment as from
reading. Surely it is better to read altogether only three
pages of a four-hundred-page book a thousand times
more thoroughly than the normal reader who reads
everything but does not read a single page thoroughly,
he said. It is better to read twelve lines of a book with

the utmost intensity and thus to penetrate into them to the full, as one might say, rather than read the whole book *as the normal reader does*, who in the end knows the book he has read no more than an air passenger knows the landscape he overflies. He does not even perceive the contours. Thus all people nowadays read everything by flying over, they read everything and know nothing. I enter into a book and settle in it, neck and crop, you should realize, in one or two pages of a philosophical essay as if I were entering a landscape, a piece of nature, a state organism, a detail of the earth, if you like, in order to penetrate into it entirely and not just with half my strength or half-heartedly, in order to explore it and then, having explored it with all the thoroughness at my disposal, drawing conclusions as to the whole. He who reads everything has understood nothing, he said. It is not necessary to read all of Goethe or all of Kant, it is not necessary to read all of Schopenhauer; a few pages of *Werther*, a few pages of *Elective Affinities* and we know more in the end about the two books than if we had read them from beginning to end, which would anyway deprive us of the purest enjoyment. But such drastic self-restraint requires so much courage and such strength of mind as can only rarely be mustered and as we ourselves muster only rarely; the reading person, just as the carnivorous, is gluttonous in the most revolting manner and, like the carnivorous person, upsets his stomach and his entire health, his head and his whole intellectual existence. We even understand a philosophical essay better if we do not gobble it up *entirely* and at one go, but pick out a detail from which we then arrive at the whole, if we are lucky. Our greatest pleasure, surely, is in fragments, just as we derive the most pleasure from life if we regard it as a fragment, whereas the whole and the complete and perfect are basically abhorrent to us. Only when we are fortunate enough to turn something whole, something complete or indeed perfect into a fragment, when we get down to reading it, only then do we experience a high degree, at times indeed a supreme degree, of pleasure in it. Our age has long been intolerable as a whole he said, only when we perceive a fragment of it is it tolerable to us. The whole and the perfect are intolerable, he said. That is why, fundamentally, all of these paintings here in the Kunsthistorisches Museum are intolerable, if I am to be honest, they are abhorrent to me. In order to be able to bear them I search for a so-called *massive mistake* in and about every single one of them, a procedure which so far has always attained its objective of turning that so-called perfect work of art into a fragment, he said. The perfect not only threatens us ceaselessly with our ruin, it also ruins everything that is hanging on these walls under the label of *masterpiece*. I proceed from the assumption that there is no such thing as the perfect or the whole, and each time I have made a fragment of one of the so-called perfect works of art hanging here on the walls by searching for a massive mistake in and about that work of art, for the crucial point of failure by the artist who made that work of art, searching for it until I found it, I have got one step further. In every one of these paintings, these so-called masterpieces, I have found and un-covered a massive mistake, the failure of its creator. For over thirty years this, as you might think, infamous calculation has come out right. Not one of these world-famous masterpieces, no matter by whom, is in fact whole or perfect. That reassures me. It makes me basically happy. Only when, time and again, we have discovered that there is no such thing as the whole or the perfect are we able to live on. We cannot endure the whole or the perfect. We have to travel to Rome to discover that Saint Peter's is a tasteless concoction, that Bernini's altar is an architectural nonsense. We have to see the Pope face to face and *personally discover* that all in all he is just as helpless and grotesque a person as anyone else in order to bear it. We have to listen to Bach and hear how he fails, listen to Beethoven and hear how he fails, even listen to Mozart and hear how he fails. And we have to deal in the same way with the so-called great philosophers, even if they are our favourite spiritual artists, he said. After all, we do not love Pascal because he is so perfect but because he is fundamentally so helpless, just as we love Montaigne for his helplessness in lifelong searching and failing to find, and Voltaire for his helplessness. We only love philosophy and the humanities generally because they are absolutely helpless. We truly love only those books which are not a whole, which are chaotic, which are helpless. The same is true of everything and everybody, Reger said, we only feel particularly attached to a person because he is helpless and not a whole, because he is chaotic and not perfect. Yes, I say, El Greco, fine, but the good man did not know how to paint a hand!, and I say Veronese, fine, but the good man of course did not know how to paint a natural face. And what I said to you about the fugue today, he was saying yesterday, not one of all the composers, even the greatest, composed a perfect one, not even Bach, who surely was tranquillity itself and pure compositional clarity. There is no perfect picture and there is no perfect book and there is no perfect piece of music, Reger said, that is the truth, and this truth makes it possible for a mind like mine, which all its life was nothing but a desperate mind, to go on existing. One's mind has to be a searching mind, a mind searching for mistakes, for the mistakes of humanity, a mind searching for failure. The human mind is a human mind only when it searches for the mistakes of humanity. The human mind is not a human mind unless it sets out to search for the mistakes of humanity, Reger said. A good mind is a mind that searches for the mistakes of humanity and an exceptional mind is a mind which finds these mistakes of humanity, and a genius's mind is a mind which, having found these mistakes, points them out and with all the means at its disposal *shows up* these mistakes. In this sense, moreover, Reger said, the always unthinkingly uttered dictum of *Seek and you shall find* is found to be true. Anyone searching in this museum for mistakes in these hundreds of so-called masterpieces will also find them, Reger said. No work in this museum is free from mistakes, I say. You may smile at this, he said, it may alarm you, and it makes me happy. And there is of course a reason why I have, for over thirty years, been going *to the Kunsthistorisches Museum* and not *to the Science Museum* across the road. He was still sitting on the settee, with his black hat on his head, quite motionless, and it was obvious that for a long time now he had been contemplating not the *White-Bearded Man* but something entirely different *behind* the *White-Bearded Man*, not Tintoretto but something far outside the museum, while I myself was admittedly regarding Reger and the *White-Bearded*

Man and yet was seeing behind it the Reger who had explained the fugues to me the day before. I had heard him explain the fugues so often before that I did not feel like listening to him attentively yesterday, and although I followed what he was saying, and it was most interesting, for instance what he had to say about Schumann's attempts at the fugue, I had been quite elsewhere with my thoughts. I saw Reger sitting on the settee and beyond it the *White-Bearded Man*, and I saw Reger once again, with even greater affection than before, trying to elucidate to me the art of the fugue, and I heard what Reger was saying and yet I was gazing into my childhood and heard the voices of my childhood, the voices of my brothers and sisters, the voice of my mother, the voices of my grandparents in the country. As a child I used to be quite happy in the country, but I was always happy back in town again, just as later and to this day I am far happier in the city than in the country. Just as I have always been far happier in art than in nature, nature has, all my life, been *uncanny* to me, while in art I have always felt *secure*. Even in my childhood, which I predominantly spent in the care of my maternal grandparents, and when, taken all in all, I was really happy, I have always felt secure and at home in the so-called world of the arts, not in nature, which I have always admired but always just as much feared, and this has not changed to this day, I do not feel at home for a moment in nature, but always so in the world of the arts, and the most secure of all in the world of music. As far as I can think back, I have loved nothing more in the world than music, I reflected, looking right through Reger, out of the museum and into my childhood. I always love these perspectives into my long-past childhood and I surrender to them totally and I exploit them in whatever way I can, may this perspective of my childhood never end, I always reflect. What kind of childhood did Reger have? I reflected, I do not know much about it, Reger is not communicative about his childhood. And Irrsigler? He does not like talking about it, nor does he like looking back to it. Towards noon more and more people come to the museum in groups, lately an extraordinary number from the East European countries, for several days running I saw groups from Soviet Georgia, driven through the gallery by Russian-speaking guides, *driven* is the right word, because these groups do not walk through the museum, they rush through it, hustled, and basically totally uninterested, totally exhausted by all the impressions which bombarded them on their journey to Vienna. Last week I observed a man from Tbilisi who had detached himself from one of the Caucasian groups and had tried to make his way through the museum on his own, a painter as it turned out, who asked me about Gainsborough; I was able to oblige him and tell him where to find Gainsborough. In the end his group had already left the museum when he approached me and asked me about the *Hotel Wandl*, where his group was accommodated. He had spent half an hour in front of the *Landscape in Suffolk* without giving his group a moment's thought, this was the first time he had been in central Europe and the first time he had seen an original Gainsborough. That Gainsborough was the high spot of his trip, he said, in surprisingly good German, before turning and leaving the museum. I had offered to help him find the *Hotel Wandl* but he had declined. A young painter, of about thirty, travels with a group to Vienna and looks at the *Landscape in Suffolk* and says that seeing the *Landscape in Suffolk* has been the high spot of his trip. This fact made me reflective the whole ensuing afternoon and well into the evening. How does that man paint in Tbilisi?, I had asked myself all that time before eventually dismissing the thought as nonsensical. Lately there have been more Italians than Frenchmen, more Englishmen than Americans visiting the Kunsthistorisches Museum. The Italians with their innate understanding of art always act as if they were initiated from birth. The French tend to walk through the museum rather bored, the English act as if they knew and had seen everything. The Russians are full of admiration. The Poles regard everything with arrogance. The Germans at the Kunsthistorisches Museum look at their catalogue all the time while they go through the rooms, and scarcely at the originals hanging on the walls, they follow the catalogue and, as they walk through the museum, crawl deeper and deeper into the catalogue until, having reached the last page of the catalogue, they have therefore reached the exit from the museum. Austrians, especially Viennese, rarely go to the Kunsthistorisches Museum if one disregards the thousands of school classes which pay their duty visit to the Kunsthistorisches Museum every year. The school classes are guided through the museum by their teachers, men or women, which has a devastating effect on the pupils because, during these visits to the Kunsthistorisches Museum, the teachers by their schoolmasterly narrow-mindedness stifle any perceptivity which these pupils may have for paintings and the men who created them. Dull-witted as they generally are, they very quickly kill in the pupils in their charge any feeling not only for painting, and the visit to the museum through which they lead their, so to speak, innocent victims as a rule, by their dull-wittedness and consequential dull-witted garrulousness, thus becomes the last visit to a museum by any of these individual pupils. Having once visited the Kunsthistorisches Museum with their teachers, these pupils never enter it again as long as they live. The first visit of all these young people is simultaneously their last. On these visits the teachers destroy for good the interest in art of the pupils in their charge, that is a fact. The teachers ruin the pupils, that is the truth, that is a century-old fact, and Austrian teachers in particular ruin in their pupils any taste for art from the start; at first all young people are receptive to everything, hence also to art, but the teachers thoroughly drive the art out of them; the predominantly dull-witted heads of Austrian teachers to this day proceed ruthlessly against their pupils' longing for art and generally for anything artistic by which all young people are initially fascinated and delighted in the most natural way. The teachers, however, are through and through *petit-bourgeois* and instinctively act against their pupils' fascination by art and enthusiasm for art by reducing art and generally anything artistic to their own depressing, stupid dilettantism and by turning art and generally anything artistic at school into their repulsive recorder playing and an equally repulsive and incompetent choral singing, which is bound to repel the pupils. Thus the teachers from the very outset block their pupils from access to art. The teachers do not know what art is, and therefore cannot explain to their pupils or teach them what art is, and they lead them not *towards* art but push them *away* from art into their revolting, sentimental vocal and instrumental *applied art*, which is bound to repel their pupils. There is no cheaper artistic taste than that of teachers. Right from primary school, teachers ruin the pupils' artistic taste, they drive all art out of their pupils from the start, instead of elucidating art, and especially music, to them and making it a lifelong joy. But then the teachers are preventers and destroyers not only in matters of art, the teachers have always, all in all, been the preventers of life and existence, instead of teaching young people how to live, of deciphering life for them, of making life for them into a truly inexhaustible wealth of their nature, they kill it in them, they do everything to kill it in them. Most of our teachers are miserable creatures whose mission in life seems to consist of barricading life to the young people and eventually and finally making it into a terrible disillusionment. After all, it is only the sentimental and perverse small minds from the lower middle class which push their way into the teaching profession. The teachers are the henchmen of the state, and seeing that this Austrian state today is a spiritually and morally totally crippled state, one which teaches nothing but brutalization and corruption and dangerous chaos, the teachers, quite naturally, are also spiritually and morally deformed and brutalized and corrupt and chaotic. This *Catholic* state has no understanding of art and hence the teachers of this state have none, or are supposed to have none, that is what is so depressing. These teachers teach what this Catholic state is and instructs them to teach: narrow-mindedness and brutality, vileness and meanness, depravity and chaos. There is nothing the pupils can expect from these teachers other than the mendacity of the Catholic state and of the Catholic state's power, I reflected while observing Reger and simultaneously, through Tintoretto's *White-Bearded Man*, gazing into my childhood. I myself had these dreadful unscrupulous teachers, first rural teachers then urban teachers, and again, in turn, urban teachers and rural teachers, and I was ruined by them well into mid-life; they ruined me for decades to come, did my teachers, I reflected. They gave me and my generation nothing but the hideousness of the state and of a world spoilt and destroyed by that state. They gave me and my generation nothing but the repulsiveness of the state and of a world marked by that state. They gave me, just as the young people of today, nothing but their *un*reason, their *in*competence, their dull-wittedness, their brainlessness. My teachers have given me nothing but their *in*competence, I consider. They have taught me nothing other than chaos. For decades ahead they have, with the utmost ruthlessness, destroyed in me everything that had originally been in me to be developed, with all the potential of my intelligence, for the sake of my world. I myself had these appalling, narrow-minded, degraded teachers who have a thoroughly low opinion of human beings and of the human world, the lowest opinion decreed by the state, namely that nature must always and regardlessly be suppressed in the new young people and eventually killed for the purposes of the state. I too had those teachers with their perverse recorder playing and their perverse guitar strumming, who forced me to learn a sixteen-stanza Schiller poem by heart, which I always felt to be one of the most terrible punishments. I too had those teachers with their secret contempt of humanity as a method *vis-à-vis* their powerless pupils, those sentimentally grandiloquent henchmen of the state with their raised forefinger. I too had those feeble-minded mediators of the state, who several times a week caned my fingers with their hazel switch until they were swollen and pulled my head up by my ears so that I never overcame my secret fits of crying. Today the teachers no longer pull ears nor do they cane pupils' fingers with hazel switches, but their sick mentality has remained the same, I see nothing changed when I watch the teachers marching past the so-called old masters with their pupils, they are the same people, I reflect, as I had, the same who ruined me for life and destroyed me for life. This is how it has to be, this is how it is, the teachers say and they do not tolerate the least opposition because the Catholic state does not tolerate the least opposition and they leave their pupils nothing, absolutely nothing, of their own. These pupils are simply force-fed with state refuse, no differently from the way geese are force-fed with maize, and the state refuse is forced into their heads until these heads are chocked. The state believes that *the children are the children of the state* and it acts accordingly and has, over the centuries, produced its devastating effect. *The state* in fact gives birth to the children, *only state children are being born*, that is the truth. There is no free child, there is only the state child, with whom the state can do what it pleases, it is the state that brings the children into this world, their mothers are merely made to believe that they bring their children into the world, but *it is the state's belly from which the children come*, that is the truth. Hundreds of thousands come out of that state belly each year, as state children, that is the truth. The state children come into the world from the state belly and they go to the state school, where they are worked on by the state teachers. The state gives birth to its children into the state, that is the truth, and it retains its hold over them. Wherever we look we see only state children, state pupils, state workers, state officials, state pensioners, state dead, that is the truth. The state produces and permits only state people, that is the truth. Natural man no longer exists, there is only state man, and where natural man still exists he is persecuted and chased to death and/or turned into state man. My childhood was to the same extent a beautiful as it was a cruel and horrid childhood, I now reflect, when, being with my grandparents, I was allowed to be a natural person, whereas at school I had to be a state person, at home with my grandparents I was a natural person, at school I was a state person, half a day I was the natural person and half a day the state person, half a day, in the afternoon, I was a natural and hence a happy person, and half a day, in the morning, I was a state person and hence unhappy. In the afternoon I was the happiest, and in the morning the unhappiest person imaginable. For many years, in the afternoons, I was the happiest person that can be, and in the mornings the unhappiest, I now reflect. With my grandparents at home I was a natural happy person, down there at school, in the provincial town, I was an unnatural unhappy person. Walking down into the provincial town I was walking into (the state's!) unhappiness, walking home towards the mountain, home to my grandparents, I was walking into happiness. Walking up the mountain to my grandparents I was walking into nature and into happiness, walking downhill into the provincial town and to school I was walking into un-nature and unhappiness. In the morning I went straight into unhappiness and at noon or in the early afternoon I returned to happiness. School is the state school, where young people are turned into state persons and thus into nothing other than henchmen of the state. Walking to school I was walking into the state and, since the state destroys people, into the institution for the destruction of people. For many years *I walked* from happiness (of grandparents) into unhappiness (of the state) and back again, from nature into un-nature and back again, my whole childhood was nothing but this toing and froing. Amidst this childhood toing and froing I grew up. But the victor in this diabolical game was not nature but *un*-nature, the school and the state, not my grandparents' home. The state forced me, like everyone else, into itself and made me compliant towards it, the state, and turned me into a state person, regulated and registered and trained and finished and perverted and dejected, like everyone else. When we see people we only see state people, the state *servants*, as we quite rightly say, who serve the state all their lives and thus serve un-nature all their lives. When we see people we only see state people as unnatural people succumbed to state dull-wittedness.

When we see people we only see people surrendered to the state and serving the state, people who have fallen victim to the state. The people we see are state victims and the humanity we see is nothing, other than state fodder with which the ever more gluttonous state is being fed. Humanity is now only state humanity and has lost its identity for centuries, in fact ever since there has been a state, I reflect. Humanity today is only an *in*humanity which is the state, I reflect. Man today is only a state man, and in consequence he is today only a destroyed man and a state man as the only humanly possible man, it seems to me. Natural man is no longer even possible, it seems to me. When we see the crowded millions of state people in the big cities we feel sick, because we also feel sick when we see the state. Every morning, as we wake up, we feel sick at this state of ours, and when we step out into the street we feel sick at the state people who populate this state. Humanity is a gigantic state which, if we are honest, makes us sick each time we wake up. Like everybody, I live in a state which makes me sick when I wake up. The teachers we have teach the state to young people, teaching them all the dreadfulness and horrors of the state, all the mendacity of the state, but they do not teach them that the state *is* all this dreadfulness and these horrors and this mendacity. For centuries the teachers have taken their pupils into the state's pincers, torturing them for years and for decades and crushing them. And here these teachers walk through the museum with their pupils, on the instruction of the state, and by their dull-wittedness ruin their taste for art. But what else is this art hanging on these walls but *state art*, it seems to me. Reger talks only of *state art* when he talks about art, *and when he talks about the so-called old masters he always only talks about the state old masters*. Because the art hanging on these walls is nothing but state art, at least that hanging here in the picture gallery of the Kunsthistorisches Museum. All the paintings hanging on these walls are nothing but paintings by state artists. *Pleasing Catholic state art, nothing else*. Always only a visage, as Reger says, never a face. Always only lineaments, never features. All in all always only the aspect without the reverse, always only lies and mendacity without reality or truth. All these painters were nothing but utterly mendacious state artists pampering to the vanity of their clients, not even Rembrandt is an exception, Reger says. Just look at Velazquez, nothing but state art, or Lotto, or Giotto, always only state art, just as that dreadful proto-Nazi and pre-Nazi Dürer, who put nature on his canvas and killed it, *this horrible Dürer*, as Reger very often says because he really hates Dürer from the depth of his soul, *this Nuremberg engraver*. State-commissioned art is what Reger calls the paintings hanging on these walls, *including even the White-Bearded Man*. The so-called old masters only ever served the state or the Church, which comes to the same thing, as Reger says time and again, they served an emperor or a Pope, a duke or an archbishop. Just as so-called free man is a utopia, so the so-called free artist has always been a utopia, Reger often says. Artists, the so-called great artists, I believe, are moreover, says Reger, the most unscrupulous of all people, they are a lot more unscrupulous even than politicians. Artists are the worst liars, even worse than the politicians, which means that the art artists are even worse liars than the state artists, I can hear Reger say again. This art invariably turns towards the all-powerful and the powerful, and away from the world, Reger often says, therein lies its baseness. This art is pitiful, no less, I can now hear Reger saying yesterday, while watching him from the Sebastiano Room today. Why do painters paint at all, when there is such a thing as nature? Reger asked himself yesterday, not for the first time. Even the most extraordinary work of art is only a pitiful, totally senseless and pointless effort to imitate nature, indeed to ape it, he said. What is Rembrandt's painted face of his mother compared with the actual face of mine? he asked again. What are the Danube meadows through which I can *walk* while I can *see* them compared to the *painted ones?* he said. *Recording,* people say, *documenting,* but, as we know, it is only the mendacious, the untrue, only falsehoods and lies that are recorded and documented, posterity has only falsehoods and lies hanging on its walls, there are only falsehoods and lies in the books which the so-called great writers have left us, only falsehoods and lies in the paintings which hang on these walls. The man hanging on the wall here is never the one the painter painted, Reger said yesterday. The man hanging on the wall is not the one who lived, he said. Of course, he said, you will say that it is *the view of the artist* who painted the picture, that is true, even though it is a mendacious view, it is, at least as far as the paintings in this museum are concerned, always only *the Catholic state view of the artist in question*, because nothing that hangs here is anything other than Catholic state art and in consequence, as I am bound to say, a base art, it can be as magnificent as it likes, it is only base Catholic state art. The so-called old masters, especially if one regards several of them alongside each other, I mean if one regards their works alongside each other, are all enthusiasts for lies, who have curried favour with Catholic state taste and sold themselves to it, Reger said. To that extent we are dealing only with a thoroughly depressing Catholic history of art, with a thoroughly depressing Catholic history of painting, which invariably found and had its subject in heaven or in hell but never on earth, he said. The painters did not paint what they ought to have painted but only what they were commissioned to paint or what earned them and brought them money or fame, he said. The painters, all these old masters, who most of the time nauseate me more than anything else and of whom I have always had a horror, he said, always only served one master and never themselves and hence humanity. They always painted a fake world, faked by them from within themselves, which they hoped would bring them money and fame; they all of them painted only in this manner, out of greed for money and out of greed for fame, not because they wanted to be painters but because they wanted fame or money, or both fame and money. In Europe they have only ever painted into the hands of a Catholic God or to his face, he said, a Catholic God and his Catholic gods. Every brush-stroke, however inspired, by these so-called old masters is a lie, he said. World decorators is what he yesterday called those he truly and profoundly hated and by whom, at the same time, he had always, throughout his miserable life, been fascinated. Religiously mendacious assistant decorators of the European Catholic rulers, that is what these old masters are, nothing else, you can see that in every dab of colour which these artists shamelessly pressed on their canvases, my dear Atzbacher, he said. Of course you are bound to say that this is the art of painting at its peak, he said yesterday, but do not forget to mention, or at least to think, at least to think for yourself, that it is also an infamous art of painting, the infamous about this art is at the same time the religious, that is what is so repulsive about it. If you post yourself, as I did the day before yesterday, in front of the Mantegna for an hour, you suddenly feel like tearing this Mantegna off the wall, because quite suddenly you perceive it as a great painted infamy. Or if you spent some time standing in front of the Biliverti or in front of the Campagnola. These people, after all, only painted in order to survive and for money and in order to end up in heaven and not in hell, which all their lives they feared above everything else, even though they were very clever but at the same time also very weak characters. The painters altogether did not have a good character, in fact they always had a very bad character and therefore, basically, also always had very bad taste, Reger said yesterday, you will not find a single so-called great painter, or let us say a so-called old master, who had a good character *and* good taste, and by a good character I mean quite simply an incorruptible character. All these artists as old masters were corruptible and that makes their art so repulsive to me. Everything they have painted and which is hanging here is repulsive to me, I often think, he said yesterday, and yet for decades I have been unable to avoid studying it. That is the most terrible thing, he said yesterday, that I find these old masters most profoundly repulsive and again and again I continue to study them. But they are repellent, that is perfectly clear, he said yesterday. The old masters, as they have now been called for centuries, only stand up to superficial viewing; *if we view them thoroughly* they gradually become diminished, and when we have studied them really and truly, and that means as thoroughly as possible for as long as possible, they dissolve, they crumble for us, leaving only a flat taste, in fact most of the time a very bad taste, in our mouths. The greatest and most significant work of art ultimately weighs heavily on our heads, as a huge lump of baseness and lies, rather as an excessively large lump of meat might weigh on our stomachs. We are fascinated by a work of art and ultimately it is ridiculous. If you take the trouble, for once, to read Goethe more intently than usual, you will ultimately find that what you read is ridiculous, no matter what it is, you only have to read it more often than usual, it will inevitably become ridiculous and even the cleverest thing is ultimately a nonsense. Alas, once you read more intently you ruin everything for yourself, everything you read. It makes no difference what you read, in the end it will become ridiculous and in the end it will be worthless. Beware of penetrating into a work of art, he said, you will ruin each and every one for yourself, even those you love most. Do not look at a picture for too long, do not read a book too intently, do not listen to a piece of music with the greatest intensity. You will ruin everything for yourself, and thus the most beautiful and the most useful things in the world. Read what you love but do not penetrate totally, listen to what you love but do not listen to it totally, look at what you love but do not look at it totally. Because I have always looked at everything totally, always listened to everything totally, always read everything totally, or at least always tried to listen to everything totally and to read and view everything totally, I ended up by ultimately making everything abhorrent to me, in this way I made all art and all music and all literature abhorrent to me, he said yesterday. As I have, by the same method, made the whole world abhorrent to me, simply everything. For years I simply made everything abhorrent to me and, what I regret most deeply, made it abhorrent to my wife too. For years, he said, I have only managed to exist by and as a result of this method of making things abhorrent. Now I know that I must not read totally or listen totally or view and contemplate totally if I want to go on living. There is an art in not reading

totally and not listening totally and not viewing totally
or looking totally, he said. I have not quite mastered
that art yet, he said, because my natural inclination is
to approach everything totally and to persevere totally
and bring it to a conclusion totally, that is, you should
know, my real misfortune, he said. For decades I
have wanted to do everything totally, that was my
misfortune, he said. This highly personal disintegrating
mechanism always focused on the total, he said. But
then the old masters did not paint for people like me,
nor did the great old composers or the great old
writers produce their works for people like me,
naturally not for people like me, never would any of
them have painted or written or composed music for
a person like me, he said. The arts are not made for
total viewing or for total listening or for total reading,
he said. This art is made for the pitiful portion of
humanity, for the everyday, for the normal, for, I am
bound to say it, the gullible portion, none other. A
great piece of architecture, he said, how quickly it is
diminished under the scrutiny of an eye such as mine,
no matter how famous it may be, and especially if it
is famous it sooner or later shrinks to a ridiculous
piece of architecture. I have travelled, he said, in order
to see great architecture, naturally first to Italy and to
Greece and to Spain, but the cathedrals always soon
shrank under my eyes to nothing but helpless, and

indeed ridiculous, attempts to juxtapose to heaven something like a *second* heaven, from one cathedral to the next always an even more magnificent *second* heaven, from one temple to the next always something even more magnificent, he said, yet the result has always been something bungled. Naturally I visited the greatest museums, and not only in Europe, and studied what they contained, with the greatest intensity, believe me, and it soon seemed to me as if these museums contained nothing but painted helplessness, painted incompetence, painted failure, the bungled part of the world, everything in these museums is failure and bungling, he said yesterday, no matter what museum you enter and get down to viewing and studying, you study nothing but failure and bungling. Very well, the Prado, he said, surely the most important museum in the world as far as the old masters are concerned, but each time I sit at the Ritz across the street, drinking my tea, I reflect that even the Prado contains only imperfect, unsuccessful, ultimately only ridiculous and dilettantish things. Some artists, he said, at certain times, when they are in vogue, are quite simply inflated to world-rousing monstrosity; then abruptly some incorruptible mind pricks that world-rousing monstrosity and the world-rousing monstrosity bursts and is nothing, just as abruptly, he said. Velazquez, Rembrandt, Giorgione,

Bach, Handel, Mozart, Goethe, he said, just as Pascal, Voltaire, all of them such inflated monstrosities. *That Stifter*, he said yesterday, an author I myself had always so enormously revered that it became more like artistic addiction, is just as bad a writer on closer examination as Bruckner, on intensive listening, is a bad if not a lousy composer. Stifter writes in a terrible style, one which grammatically is beneath contempt, and Bruckner has similarly slipped the reins with his chaotically wild, and even in old age, religiously pubertal intoxication of sounds. I have revered Stifter for decades without actually concerning myself with him accurately or radically. When, about a year ago, I did concern myself accurately and radically with Stifter, I could not believe my eyes and ears. Such faulty and bungled German or Austrian, whichever you prefer, I had never before read in my whole intellectual life in an author who is, of all things, famous today for his precise and clear prose. Stifter's prose is anything but precise and it is the least clear I have come across, it is packed with distorted metaphors and faulty and confused ideas, and I really wonder why this provincial dilettante, who at any rate was an inspector of schools in Upper Austria, is today revered to such an extent by writers, and above all by the younger writers, and not by any means by the least known or least noticed ones. I believe that none of these people has ever really read Stifter but they have always only venerated him blindly, that they have always only heard of him but never really read him, like myself. As I was truly reading Stifter a year ago, that *grandmaster of prose writing*, as he is called, I felt disgusted with myself for ever having revered this bungler of a writer, or indeed loved him. I had read Stifter in my youth and my memory of him had been based on these reading experiences. I had read Stifter between the ages of twelve and sixteen, at a time when I was totally uncritical. After that I never re-examined Stifter. For very long stretches of his prose Stifter is an unbearable chatterbox, he has an incompetent and, which is most despicable, a slovenly style and he is moreover, in actual fact, the most boring and mendacious author in the whole of German literature. Stifter's prose, which is reputed to be pregnant and precise, is in fact woolly, helpless and irresponsible, and pervaded by a *petit-bourgeois* sentimentality and a *petit-bourgeois* gaucherie that turns one's stomach at the reading of *Witiko* or *The Papers of My Great-grandfather*. *The Papers of My Great-grandfather*, in particular, is, from the very first few lines, an attempt to present a recklessly spun-out, sentimental and boring prose full of internal and external mistakes as a work of art, when it is nothing but a *petit-bourgeois* concoction from Linz. But then it would be quite inconceivable that a *petit-bourgeois* provincial dump like Linz, which has, since the days of Kepler, remained a provincial hole veritably crying out to high heaven, which has an opera house where they cannot sing, a theatre where they cannot act, painters who cannot paint and writers who cannot write, should suddenly give birth to a genius – and Stifter is universally described as one. Stifter is no genius, Stifter is a philistine living a cramped life and a musty *petit bourgeois* and schoolmaster writing in a cramped style, who did not even meet the minimum requirements of the language, let alone was able to produce works of art, Reger said. All in all, he said, Stifter is one of the greatest disappointments of my artistic life. Every third or at least every fourth sentence of Stifter's is wrong, every other or every third metaphor is a failure, and Stifter's mind generally, at least in his literary writings, is a mediocre mind. Stifter in fact is one of the most unimaginative writers who ever wrote anything and one of the most anti-poetical and unpoetical ones to boot. But readers and literary scholars have always been taken in by that man Stifter. The fact that the man, towards the end of his life, killed himself changes nothing about his absolute mediocrity. I do not know any writer in the world who is such a dilettante and a bungler, and moreover so blinkered and narrow-minded as Stifter, and so world-famous at the same time. Things are much the same with Anton Bruckner, Reger said; with his perverse fear of God and his obsession with Catholicism he left Upper Austria for Vienna and totally surrendered himself to the emperor and to God. Bruckner was no genius either. His music is confused and just as unclear and bungled as Stifter's prose. But whereas Stifter today, strictly speaking, is only the dead paper of German literary scholars, Bruckner is moving everyone to tears. Bruckner's surge of sound has conquered the world, one might say, sentimentality and false pompousness are celebrating triumphs with Bruckner. Bruckner is just as slovenly a composer as Stifter is a slovenly writer, both of them share that Upper Austrian slovenliness. Both of them make so-called devout art which in fact is a public danger, Reger said. Kepler, of course, was quite a lad, Reger said yesterday, but then he was no Upper Austrian but from Württemberg; Adalbert Stifter and Anton Bruckner ultimately only produced literary and musical refuse. Anyone appreciating Bach and Mozart, and Handel and Haydn, he said, must reject people like Bruckner as a matter of course, he need not despise them, but he must reject them. And anyone appreciating Goethe and Kleist and Novalis and Schopenhauer, must reject Stifter but he need not despise Stifter. Whoever loves Goethe cannot at the same time love Stifter, Goethe made things difficult for himself, Stifter always made them too easy for himself. The most despicable thing, Reger said yesterday, is that Stifter, of all people, was a feared school official, moreover a school official in a superior position, and that he wrote in such a slovenly manner as none of his pupils would have been allowed to get away with. One page of Stifter, submitted to Stifter by one of his pupils, would have been totally massacred by Stifter with his red pencil, he said, that is the truth. Once we start reading Stifter with a red pencil there is no end to our correcting mistakes, Reger said. This is not a genius taking up his pen but a woeful incompetent. If ever there was such a concept as tasteless, dull and sentimental and pointless literature, then it applies exactly to what Stifter has written. Stifter's writing is no art, and what he has to say is dishonest in the most revolting fashion. It is not for nothing that Stifter is read mainly in their homes by the wives and widows of officials yawning with boredom at the passage of their day, he said, and by nurses during off-duty hours and by nuns in their convents. A genuinely thinking person cannot read Stifter. I believe that the people who estimate Stifter so highly, so enormously highly, have no idea of Stifter. All our writers nowadays, without exception, speak and write enthusiastically about Stifter and follow him as if he were the literary god of the present age. Either these people are stupid and lack all appreciation of art, or else they do not understand anything about literature, or else, which unfortunately I am bound to believe, they never read Stifter, he said. You must not talk to me about Stifter or Bruckner, he said, certainly not in connection with art or with what I understand by art. The one is a prose blurrer, he said, the other a music blurrer. Poor Upper Austria, he said, really believing that it has produced two of the greatest geniuses, while in fact it has produced only two boundlessly overrated duds, one literary and the other musical. When I consider how the Austrian schoolmistresses and nuns have their Stifter lying on their bedside tables, as an art icon, next to their combs and next to their toe-nail clippers, and when I consider how the heads of state burst into tears while listening to a Bruckner symphony, I feel quite sick, he said. Art is the most sublime and the most revolting thing simultaneously, he said. But we must make ourselves believe that there is high art and the highest art, he said, otherwise we should despair. Even though we know that all art ends in gaucherie and in ludicrousness and in the refuse of history, like everything else, we must, with *downright self-assurance*, believe in high and in the highest art, he said. We realize what it is, a bungled, failed art, but we need not always hold this realization before us, because in that case we should inevitably perish, he said. To return to Stifter once more, he said, there are a large number of writers today who invoke Stifter. These writers invoke an absolute dilettante writer who throughout his life as a writer has done nothing but abuse nature. Stifter can be accused of absolute abuse of nature, Reger said yesterday. He wanted to be a seer as a writer but in actual fact he was a blind man as a writer, Reger said. Everything about Stifter is officious, virginally gawky; Stifter wrote an unbearable provincial raised-finger kind of prose, Reger said, nothing else. Stifter's descriptions of nature are always extolled. Never has nature been so misconstrued as in Stifter's descriptions, nor indeed is it as boring as he makes us believe on his patient pages, Reger said. Stifter is nothing but a literary fusspot whose artless pen paralyses nature and hence also the reader, where in reality and in truth nature is vital and eventful. Stifter covered everything with his *petit-bourgeois* veil and all but stifled it, that is the truth. In reality he cannot describe a tree, nor a song bird, nor a torrential river, that is the truth. He tries to bring something to life for us and only paralyses it, he wants to produce brilliance and only dulls it, that is the truth. Stifter makes nature monotonous and his characters insensitive and insipid, he knows nothing and he invents nothing, and what he describes, because he is solely a describer and nothing else, he describes with boundless naïveté. He has the quality of poor painters, Reger says, who for God knows what reasons have come to fame and who are hanging on the walls everywhere also in this institution, you need only think of Dürer and of those hundreds of mediocre products of which their frames are worth a lot more than they are. All these paintings are admired, but the admirers do not know why, just as Stifter is read and admired without his readers knowing why. The most mysterious thing about Stifter is his fame, Reger said, because his literature is anything but mysterious. As for the so-called great ones, we dissolve them, disintegrate them in time, and reduce them, he said, the great painters, the great musicians, the great writers, because we cannot live with their greatness, because we think, and think everything through to the end, he said. But Stifter was and is not great and therefore he is no example of this process. Stifter is merely an example of an artist being venerated as great for decades, and indeed loved, by a person, in fact by a person *addicted* to veneration and love, without ever having been great. In the disillusionment we experience upon discovering that the greatness of the one we have venerated and loved is no greatness at all and never was such greatness, but only an imagined greatness and is in fact pettiness, and indeed baseness, we experience the merciless pangs of the deceived. We quite simply pay the price, Reger said, for having lent ourselves to blindly accepting an object, moreover for years and decades and possibly for a lifetime, and even to venerating and loving it, without time and again putting it to the test. If only, let us say, thirty or even twenty years ago, or fifteen years ago, I had put Stifter to the test I should have saved myself this late disappointment. Altogether we should never say this or that person is the thing, and will then remain the thing for all time, we should again and again put all artists to the test, because we keep developing our art scholarship and our artistic taste, that is unquestionable. The only good thing by Stifter are his letters, Reger said, everything else is worthless. But literary scholarship will no doubt continue to concern itself with Stifter for a long time to come, after all it is obsessed by such literary idols as Adalbert Stifter who, even if they do not go down into *eternal prose*, will long help these scholars to earn their crust of bread in the most agreeable way. Once or twice I took the trouble of giving various people, very clever and less clever people, very perceptive ones and less perceptive ones, a book by Stifter to read, such as *Colourful Stones, The Condor* or *Brigitta*, or those *Papers of My Great-grandfather*, and then questioned those people as to whether they had liked what they had read, demanding an honest answer. And all these people, compelled by me to give an honest answer, told me they had *not* liked it, that they had been *infinitely disappointed*, that basically it had said nothing, but absolutely nothing, to them, they were all simply amazed that a person who wrote such brainless works, and moreover had nothing to communicate, could become so famous. That *Stifter experiment* amused me again and again for some time, he said, the fact that I conducted this *Stifter test*, as I called it. In exactly the same way I sometimes ask people if they really like Titian, for instance the *Madonna with the Cherries*. Not a single person I asked ever liked the picture, they all admired it solely because of its fame, it did not really say anything to any of them. But I do not wish to say that I am likening Stifter to Titian, that would be quite absurd, Reger said. The literary scholars are not only infatuated with Stifter, they are crazy about Stifter. I think the literary scholars apply an absolutely inadequate yardstick where Stifter is concerned. They write more about Stifter than about any other author of his period, and when we read *what* they write about Stifter we have to assume that they have either read nothing of Stifter or else have read everything only quite superficially. Nature is now enjoying a boom, Reger said yesterday, that is why Stifter is now enjoying a boom. Anything to do with nature is now very much in vogue, Reger said yesterday, that is why Stifter is now greatly, or more than greatly, in vogue. The forest is now greatly in vogue, mountain streams are now greatly in vogue. Stifter bores everybody to death yet in some fatal manner is now greatly in vogue, Reger said. Sentimentality altogether, that is the terrible thing, is now greatly in vogue, just as everything else that is kitsch is now greatly in vogue; from the mid-seventies to this day in the mid-eighties sentimentality and kitsch have been greatly in vogue – greatly in vogue in literature, in painting, and also in music. Never before has so much sentimental kitsch been written as now in the eighties, never before has there been so much kitschy *and* sentimental painting, and the composers are vying with each other in kitsch and sentimentality; you only need go to the theatre, where nothing is staged nowadays except dangerous kitsch, nothing except sentimentality, and even when there is brutality and savagery on the stage it is still nothing but common kitschy sentimentality. You need only go to an exhibition and all that is shown to you there is extreme kitsch and the most revolting sentimentality. You need only go to the concert halls, and there too you will hear nothing but kitsch and sentimentality. The books today are crammed full of kitsch and sentimentality, that is what made Stifter so fashionable in recent years. Stifter is a master of kitsch,

Reger said. On any page of Stifter that you care to pick there is so much kitsch that several generations of poetry-hungry nuns and nurses can be satiated with it, he said. And in actual fact Bruckner too is nothing but sentimental and kitschy, nothing but stupid, monumental orchestrated sickly ear-wax. The young and the very young writers working today mostly write nothing but brainless and mindless kitsch and in their books they develop a positively unbearable bombastic sentimentality, it is therefore easy to understand why Stifter is the height of fashion for them too. Stifter, who introduced brainless and mindless kitsch into great and noble literature and who ended up committing a kitschy suicide, is now the height of fashion, Reger said. It is by no means incomprehensible that just now, when the word *forest* and the word *forest death*, have so much come into vogue, and when altogether the *notion of forest* is the most used and the most *mis*used notion of all, Stifter's *Tall Forest* is being bought in greater numbers than ever before. People today yearn for *nature* more than they have done ever before, and because everyone believes that Stifter has described nature they all run to Stifter. But Stifter has not described nature at all, he has only kitschified it. The whole stupidity of people is revealed in the fact that they are all now making pilgrimages to Stifter, in their hundreds of thousands, kneeling down before every one of his books as if every one of them were an altar. It is in this kind of pseudo-enthusiasm, more than in anything else, that I find humanity distasteful, Reger said, I find it absolutely repulsive. In the end everything eventually becomes a prey to ridicule or at least to triviality, no matter how great and important it may be. Stifter in fact always reminds me of *Heidegger*, of that ridiculous Nazi philistine in plus-fours. Just as Stifter has totally and in the most shameless manner kitschified great literature, so Heidegger, the Black Forest philosopher Heidegger, has kitschified philosophy, Heidegger and Stifter, each one for himself and in his own way, have hopelessly kitschified philosophy and literature. Heidegger, after whom the wartime and postwar generations have been chasing, showering him with revolting and stupid doctoral theses even in his lifetime – I always visualize him sitting on his wooden bench outside his Black Forest house, alongside his wife who, with her perverse knitting enthusiasm, ceaselessly knits winter socks for him from the wool she has herself shorn from their own Heidegger sheep. I cannot visualize Heidegger other than sitting on the bench outside his Black Forest house, alongside his wife, who all her life totally dominated him and who knitted all his socks and crocheted all his caps and baked all his bread and wove all his bedlinen and who even cobbled up his sandals for him. Heidegger was a kitschy brain, Reger said, just as Stifter, but actually a lot more ridiculous than Stifter who in fact was *a tragic figure* unlike Heidegger, who was *always merely comical*, just as *petit-bourgeois* as Stifter, just as disastrously megalomaniac, a feeble thinker from the Alpine foothills, as I believe, and just about right for the German philosophical hot-pot. For decades they ravenously spooned up that man Heidegger, more than anybody else, and overloaded their German philological and philosophical stomachs with his stuff. Heidegger had a common face, not a spiritual one, Reger said, he was through and through an unspiritual person, devoid of all fantasy, devoid of all sensibility, a genuine German philosophical ruminant, a ceaselessly gravid German philosophical cow, Reger said, which grazed upon German philosophy and thereupon for decades let its smart little cowpats drop on it. Heidegger, in a manner of speaking, was a philosophical con-man, Reger said, who succeeded in getting a whole generation of German philosophers to stand on their heads. Heidegger is a revolting episode in the history of German philosophy, Reger said yesterday, an episode in which all philosophical Germans participated and *still participate*. To this day Heidegger has still not been entirely exposed for what he is; true, the Heidegger cow has become thinner but the Heidegger cow is still being milked. Heidegger in his worn plus-fours in front of that lie of a log cabin at Todtnauberg is all I have left as an unmasking photograph, the philosophical philistine with his crocheted black Black Forest cap on his head, under which, when all is said and done, nothing but German feeble-mindedness is warmed up over and over again, Reger said. By the time we are old we have undergone a great many murderous fashions, all those murderous fashions in art and in philosophy and in consumer goods. Heidegger is a good example of how nothing is left of a fashion in philosophy which at one time had gripped the whole of Germany, nothing left but a number of ridiculous photographs and a number of even more ridiculous writings. Heidegger was a philosophical market crier who only brought stolen goods to the market, everything of Heidegger's is second-hand, he was and is the prototype of the *re*-thinker, who lacked everything, but truly every-thing, for independent thinking. Heidegger's method, consisted in the most unscrupulous turning of other people's great ideas into small ideas of his own, that is a fact. Heidegger has so reduced everything great that it has become *German-compatible*, you understand: *German-compatible*, Reger said. Heidegger is the *petit bourgeois* of German philosophy, the man who has placed on German philosophy his kitschy night-cap, that kitschy black night-cap which Heidegger always wore, on all occasions. Heidegger is the carpet-slipper and night-cap philosopher of the Germans, nothing else. I don't know why, Reger said yesterday, whenever I think of Stifter I also think of Heidegger and the other way about. Surely it is no accident, Reger said, that Heidegger just as Stifter has always been popular, and is still popular, mainly with those tense women, and just as those fussy do-gooding nuns and those fussy do-gooding nurses devour Stifter as their favourite dish, in a manner of speaking, so they also devour Heidegger. Heidegger to this day is the favourite philosopher of German womanhood. Heidegger is *the women's philosopher*, the specially suitable luncheon philosopher straight from the scholars' frying pan. When you come to a *petit-bourgeois* or even an aristocratic-*petit-bourgeois* party, you are very often served Heidegger even before the hors-d'oeuvre, you have not even taken off your overcoat and already you are being offered a piece of Heidegger, you have not even sat down and already the lady of the house has brought Heidegger in with the sherry on a silver salver. Heidegger is invariably a well-cooked German philosophy which may be served anywhere and at any time, Reger said, in any household. I do not know of any philosopher today who has been more degraded, Reger said. Anyway, Heidegger is finished as far as philosophy is concerned, whereas ten years ago he was still the great thinker, he now, as it were, only haunts pseudo-intellectual households and pseudo-intellectual parties, adding an artificial mendaciousness to their entirely natural one. Like Stifter, Heidegger is a tasteless and readily digestible reader's pudding for the mediocre German mind. Heidegger has no more to do with intellect than Stifter has with poetry, believe me, and as far as philosophy and poetry are concerned, the two of them are worth nothing, although I still value Stifter more highly than Heidegger, who has always repelled me, because everything about Heidegger has always been repulsive to me, not only the night-cap on his head and his homespun winter long-johns above the stove which he himself had lit at Todtnauberg, not only his Black Forest walking stick which he himself had whittled, in fact his entire hand-whittled Black Forest philosophy, everything about that tragicomical man has always been repulsive to me, has always profoundly repulsed me whenever I even thought of it; I only had to know a single line of Heidegger to feel repulsed, let alone when reading Heidegger, Reger said; I have always thought of Heidegger as a charlatan who merely utilized everything around him and who, during that utilization, sunned himself on his bench at Todtnauberg. When I think that even super-intelligent people have been taken in by Heidegger and that even one of my best women friends wrote a dissertation about Heidegger, and moreover wrote that dissertation *quite seriously*, I feel sick to this day, Reger said. His *nothing is without reason* is the most ludicrous thing ever, Reger said. But the Germans are impressed by posturing, Reger said, the Germans have an *interest in posturing*, that is one of their most striking characteristics. And as for the Austrians, they are a lot worse still in all these respects. I have seen a series of photographs which a supremely talented woman photographer made of Heidegger, who in all of them looked like a retired bloated staff officer, Reger said; in these photographs Heidegger is just climbing out of bed, or Heidegger is climbing into bed, or Heidegger is sleeping, or waking up, putting on his underpants, pulling on his socks, taking a nip of grapejuice, stepping out of his log cabin and looking towards the horizon, whittling away at his stick, putting on his cap, taking off his cap, holding his cap in his hands, opening out his legs, raising his head, lowering his head, putting his right hand in his wife's left hand while his wife is putting her left hand in his right hand, walking in front of his house, walking at the back of his house, walking towards his house, walking away from his house, reading, eating, spooning his soup, cutting a slice of bread (baked by himself), opening a book (written by himself), closing a book (written by himself), bending down, straightening up, and so on, Reger said. Enough to make you throw up. If even the Wagnerians are more than flesh and blood can bear, what about the Heideggerians, Reger said. But of course Heidegger cannot be compared to Wagner, who really was a genius, a man to whom the *concept of genius* really applies more than to anyone else, whereas Heidegger has always only been a small philosophical rear-rank man. Heidegger, that much is clear, was the most pampered German philosopher of the century, and simultaneously the most insignificant. The people who made pilgrimages to Heidegger were mainly those who confused philosophy with culinary science, who regarded philosophy as something fried and roasted and cooked, which is entirely in line with German taste. Heidegger used to hold court at Todtnauberg and at all times would allow himself to be admired on his philosophical Black Forest plinth like a sacred cow. Even a famous and much-feared North German publisher of periodicals kneeled before him devotionally and open-mouthed, as though, in a manner of speaking, he was expecting the host of the spirit from Heidegger sitting there under the setting sun on his bench before his house. All these people made their pilgrimages to Todtnauberg to see Heidegger and made themselves look ridiculous, Reger said. They made their pilgrimages, as it were, into the philosophical Black Forest, to the sacred Mount Heidegger and knelt down before their idol. That their idol was a total spiritual wash-out – that they could not know with their dull-wittedness. They did not even suspect it, Reger said. Nevertheless the Heidegger episode is revealing as an example of the German cult of philosophers. They invariably cling to the false ones, Reger said, to those who suit them best, to the stupid and the suspect ones. But the most terrible thing is that I am related to both of them, to Stifter on my mother's side and to Heidegger on my father's side, that is positively grotesque, Reger said yesterday. I am even related to Bruckner, even though in a very round-about way, as the saying goes, but related nonetheless. Needless to say, I am not so stupid as to feel ashamed of these connections, that would be the most stupid thing of all, Reger said, even though I am not necessarily as delighted about these connections as my parents always were or as my family always was. Most of my ancestors, no matter from what Upper Austrian, or generally Austrian or German *line*, were merchants, industrialists like my father, peasants of course at an earlier time, more often from Bohemia than from anywhere else, not so much from the Alps, more from the Alpine foothills, and there was also a massive Jewish contribution. Among my ancestors there was even an archbishop and a double murderer. No way, I have always told myself, will I investigate my origins in any greater detail, who knows what even more frightful horrors I might unearth, and I confess that that frightens me. People are unearthing their ancestors and rummage and rummage in their pile of ancestors until they have rummaged it all over and they finish up even more dissatisfied and doubly dismayed and desperate, he said. I have never been a so-called ancestor rummager, I lack the necessary disposition for that, but even a person like me does incidentally come across the strangest specimens of ancestors, this is something no one escapes, no matter how much he resists that so-called exhumation of ancestors, he keeps on digging. All in all I have come from an *exceedingly interesting mixture, a cross-section, as it were, of everything that I am.* To know less than I do know would have been better in this respect, but age inevitably brings a lot to the light of day, uninvited, he said. The one I like best is the joiner's apprentice who in eighteen forty-eight learned to read and write at Cattaro and in a letter proudly informed his parents in Linz of the fact, he said. This joiner's apprentice, on my mother's side, was stationed as a gunner at the fortress of Cattaro, present-day Kotor, and I still possess that letter which he, at eighteen it is said, radiant with joy, wrote from Cattaro to his parents in Linz, and on which

there is a note from the official imperial post office
to the effect that its *content is objectionable*. We are
everything that was in our ancestors, absolutely
everything, plus what is in ourselves. To be related to
Stifter has been a precious enormity to me all my life,
until I discovered that Stifter was not the great writer
or poet, whichever, whom I had venerated all my life.
That I am related to Heidegger I have always known
because my parents let it out at every opportunity.
We are related to Stifter, and we are also related to
Heidegger, and to Bruckner too, my parents would
say at every opportunity, so much so that I often felt
embarrassed. To be related to Stifter people always
regard as something quite fantastic, certainly in Upper
Austria but also throughout Austria, and it counts at
least as much in society as if someone were to say that
he was related to the Emperor Francis Joseph, but to
be related to Stifter *and* to Heidegger, that is the most
extraordinary and the most amazing thing that one
can imagine in Austria, and indeed also in Germany.
And if, at a suitable moment, Reger said, you then add
that you are related to Bruckner too, the people simply
cannot recover from their amazement. To have a
famous poet among one's relatives is already something special, but to have also a famous philosopher
among one's relatives is of course even more fantastic,
Reger said, and on top of it to be related to Anton

Bruckner is the ultimate. My parents often mentioned this fact and of course derived advantage from it. The only crucial thing, however, was to mention these relationships in the right place; of course it goes without saying that they spoke of their relative Adalbert Stifter whenever they sought an Upper Austrian advantage, for instance from the provincial government on which every Upper Austrian is time and again dependent, or that Anton Bruckner was invoked chiefly when they had a problem in Vienna, Reger said; in the event of a Linz or Wels or Eferdingen problem, that is to say an Upper Austrian problem, they of course mentioned that they were related to Stifter; if they had a Vienna problem they would say that Bruckner was a relative of theirs, and when they were travelling through Germany they would say, a hundred times a day, that Heidegger was a relative of theirs, and they would always say that Heidegger was *a close relative* of theirs, without honestly stating how closely Heidegger was actually related to them, because in fact Heidegger is related to them and hence also to me, albeit, as the phrase is, *very distantly*. To Stifter, on the other hand, we are related *very closely* and to Bruckner also *fairly closely*, Reger said yesterday. That they were also related to a double murderer who spent the first half of his adult life in Stein-on-Danube and the second half in Garsten near Steyr, which are the two biggest Austrian penal establishments – that, needless to say, they never mentioned, although they should have invariably mentioned it in the same way. I myself have never shrunk from saying that one of my relatives had been a prisoner in Stein and in Garsten, which is probably the worst thing an Austrian can say about his relatives, on the contrary, I have mentioned the fact more often than would have been necessary, which of course can also be interpreted as a character flaw, Reger said. Similarly I never concealed the fact that I have tuberculosis and that I have always had tuberculosis, he said, and I have never in my life been afraid of this flaw or weakness. I have very often said that I am related to Stifter and to Heidegger and to Bruckner and to a double murderer who served his sentence in Steyr and in Stein, even when I was not asked about it, Reger said yesterday. We have to live with our relationships, no matter what they are, he said. After all, we *are* those relationships, he said, *within myself I am all those relatives combined.* Reger loves fog and gloom, he shies away from light, that is why he goes to the Kunsthistorisches Museum and that is also why he goes to the Ambassador, because at the Kunsthistorisches Museum it is just as gloomy as at the Ambassador, and while in the mornings he can, at the Kunsthistorisches Museum, enjoy his ideal temperature of eighteen degrees Celsius, he enjoys his ideal afternoon temperature of twenty-three degrees Celsius at the Ambassador, quite apart from anything else that, as he puts it, suits him at the Kunsthistorisches Museum on the one hand and at the Ambassador on the other. The sun can no more penetrate into the Kunsthistorisches Museum than it can into the Ambassador, that is as he likes it, because he does not like solar radiation. He avoids the sun, there is nothing he shuns more than the sun. *I hate the sun, you know that I hate the sun more than anything in the world*, he says. What he likes best are foggy days, on foggy days he leaves the house very early in the morning, actually takes a walk, which he does not normally do, for basically he hates walking. I hate walking, he says, it seems so pointless to me. I walk, and while I am walking I keep thinking how I hate walking, I have no other thoughts at the time, I cannot understand that there are people who are able to think while walking, to think of something other than that walking is pointless and useless, he says. I prefer to walk up and down in my room, it is then that I have my best ideas. I can stand by the window for hours, looking down into the street, that is a habit I acquired in childhood. I look down into the street and observe the people and ask myself who are these people, and what is moving them down there in the street, what keeps them going, that, as it were, is my principal occupation. I have always exclusively concerned myself with people, nature as such has never interested me, everything in me was always related to human beings, I am, you might say, a fanatic for human beings, he said, naturally not a fanatic for humanity but a fanatic for human beings. I have always only been interested in human beings, he said, because in the nature of things they repelled me, I have never been attracted more intensively by anything than by human beings and at the same time never more thoroughly repelled by anything than by human beings. I loathe people but they are, simultaneously, the sole purpose of my life. When I get home from a concert at night I very often stand by my window until about one or two in the morning, looking down into the street and observing the human beings passing there below. During that observation I gradually develop my work. I stand by the window, looking down into the street, and at the same time I work on my essay. Towards two in the morning I do not, as you might think, go to bed but I sit down at my desk and write my essay. I go to bed around three in the morning but I get up again about half-past seven. At my age, of course, I no longer need a lot of sleep. Sometimes I sleep for only three or four hours, that is quite sufficient. *Everybody has his bread-giver*, he said hypocritically, *my bread-giver is The Times*. It is good to have a bread-giver, it is even better to *have a secret bread-giver. The Times* is my secret master, he said yesterday. I had been observing him for a long time now without actually seeing him. He said yesterday that naturally he did not have every opportunity but certainly a great many opportunities in his childhood, and during his youth which followed upon his childhood, and that in the end he had not decided in favour of any one of those opportunities as a professional career. As he had been under no compulsion to earn a living, since what he had inherited from his parents was not to be under-rated; he had for many years, undisturbed, followed only his ideas, his predilections, his inclinations. From the outset it had not been nature that attracted him, on the contrary, he had avoided nature whenever he could do so, art had attracted him, *anything artificial,* he said yesterday, *absolutely anything artificial.* Painting had disappointed him at an early stage, from the outset it had seemed to him the unspiritual among the arts. He read a lot, and passionately, but the idea of writing himself never occurred to him, he did not think he could do it. He loved music from the outset, it was in music that he eventually found what he had missed in painting and also in literature. I certainly do not come from a musical family, he said, on the contrary, my people were all unmusical and altogether completely hostile to the arts. Only after my parents died was I able to indulge in my first predilection. My parents had to be dead for me to be able to do what I wanted to do, they had always blocked my access to my predilections, to my passions. My father was an unmusical person, he said, my mother was musical, as I believe, even highly musical, but her husband over the years had *driven* her musicality *out of her*. My parents were a *frightful couple*, he said, they secretly hated one another but were unable to separate. Possessions and money held them together, that is the truth. We had many beautiful, expensive paintings hanging on our walls, he said, but they never looked at them once in all those decades, we had many thousands of books on our shelves but they never read a single one of those books in all those decades, we had a Bösendorfer grand piano standing there but for decades no one had played it. If the lid of the piano had been welded shut they would not have noticed it for decades, he said. My parents had ears but they heard nothing, they had eyes but they saw nothing, they probably had hearts but they felt nothing. Amidst that chill I grew up, he said. I did not suffer any hardship, but even so I was in the depths of despair every single day, he said. My whole childhood was nothing but a period of despair. My parents did not love me and I did not love them. They never forgave me for having made me, all their lives they never forgave me for having made me. If there is a hell, and of course there is a hell, he said, then my childhood was that hell. Childhood probably always is hell, childhood is *the* hell, he said, no matter what kind of childhood, it is hell. People say they had a happy childhood, but it was hell all the same. People falsify everything, they also falsify the childhood they had. They say they had a happy childhood, and yet they lived through hell. The older people become the more readily they say they had a happy childhood when it cannot have been anything other than hell. *Hell does not lie ahead, hell is behind us*, he said, *because hell is childhood*. What it cost me to escape from that hell! he said yesterday. While my parents were alive it was hell for me. My parents blocked everything within me and about me, he said. In a ceaseless mechanism of suppression they nearly protected me to death, he said. My parents had to be dead for me to be able to live, when my parents died I revived. In the end it was actually music that vivified me, he said yesterday. But of course I did not wish, nor was I able, to be a creative or even a performing artist, at least not a creative or performing musical artist, but only a *critical* one. *I am a critical artist*, he said, I have been a critical artist all my life. Even in childhood I was a critical artist, he said, the circumstances of my childhood made me a critical artist in an entirely natural way. I certainly regard myself as an artist, that is as a critical artist, and as a critical artist I am of course also creative, that is obvious, hence a *performing and creative critical artist*, he said. What is more, a creative and performing critical artist of *The Times*, he said. I certainly regard my brief reports for *The Times* as works of art, and I think that as the author of these works of art I am always in one person and simultaneously a painter and a musician and a writer. That is my greatest delight: to know that as the author of these works of art for *The Times* I am a painter and a musician and a writer in one, that is my *greatest* delight. I am not therefore, as the painters are, only a painter, and I am not, as the musicians are, only a musician, and I am not, as the writers are, only a writer, you must understand that *I am a painter and a musician and a writer all in one*. That is what I perceive to be the greatest happiness, he said, to be *an artist in all the arts* and yet reside in one of them. It is possible, he said, that the critical artist is the one who practises his own art in all the arts and is aware of it, utterly and totally aware of it. This awareness makes me happy. To that extent I have been happy for over thirty years, he said, even though by nature I am an unhappy person. A thinking person is by nature an unhappy person, he said yesterday. But even that unhappy person can be happy, he said, time and again, in the truest meaning of the word and of the concept *as a diversion*. Childhood is the black hole into which one was thrust by one's parents and from which one must climb out unaided. Most people never succeed in getting out of that black hole which is their childhood, all their lives they are in that black hole, they cannot get out and they become embittered. That is why most people are embittered who fail to get out of the hole of their childhood. It certainly calls for a superhuman effort to get out of the hole of childhood. And unless we get out of that blackest of holes at an early stage we never get out of it at all, he said. My parents had to be dead for me to get out of that blackest hole of my childhood, he said, they had to be *definitely dead, in fact for ever*, you understand, for me to get out of the hole of my childhood. What my parents would have liked best was, immediately after my birth, to have locked me up in their safe along with their jewellery and their bonds, he said. I had embittered parents, he said, who suffered all their lives from their bitterness. In all the pictures I have of my parents, and whenever I look at them, I see their bitterness. There are practically no other children than children of embittered parents, that is why all parents look so embittered. All these faces are marked by bitterness and disappointment, you scarcely find any that are not, you may walk through Vienna for hours on end, for instance, and all you see in those faces is bitterness and disappointment, and things are no different out in the country, the country faces too are full of bitterness and disappointment. My parents made me, and when they saw *what* they had made they had a shock and would have preferred to unmake me. And as they could not put me in their safe they thrust me into that black hole of childhood, from which I could not emerge while they were alive. Parents invariably produce their children in an irresponsible manner, and when they see what they have produced they have a shock, that is why, whenever children are born, we see only shocked parents. To produce a child and, as the hypocritical phrase goes, bring it into the world is nothing other than bringing grave unhappiness into the world and it is this grave unhappiness that always shocks them anew. Nature has ever made fools of parents, he said, and out of these fools it produces unhappy children in dark holes of childhood. Without any embarrassment people say they have had a happy childhood, whereas in fact they had an unhappy one, from which they only escaped by a supreme effort, and for *this* reason they say they had a happy childhood, because they have escaped from the hell of childhood. To have escaped from one's childhood is nothing other than to have escaped from hell, and then people say they had a happy childhood in order to spare their

progenitors, their parents, who should not be spared.
To say that one has had a happy childhood in order
to spare one's parents is nothing but a piece of socio-
political villainy, he said. We spare our parents
instead of charging them, lifelong, with the crime of
procreation of humans, he said yesterday. For thirty-
five years they oppressed me with any means possible,
they tortured me with their frightful methods. I have
no need to give my parents the slightest consideration,
he said, they do not deserve the slightest consideration. They committed two crimes against me, two
most serious crimes, he said, they procreated me and
they oppressed me, they committed the crime of procreation against me and the crime of oppression. And
they thrust me into the black hole of childhood with
the greatest possible parental ruthlessness. As you are
aware, I had a sister who died young, he said, who
escaped our parents only by her premature death,
she had been treated by our parents with the same
ruthlessness, they oppressed me and my sister by their
trauma of disappointment, my sister did not endure
it for long and died suddenly on an April day, totally
unexpectedly, in a way that is possible only with
juveniles, she was nineteen, she died of a so-called
sudden heart attack, you understand, while my mother
on the first floor was getting everything ready for my
father's birthday party, rushing this way and that to

make quite sure no birthday mistake was made, with all kinds of plates and glasses and napkins and small cakes, nearly driving me and my sister out of our minds with her birthday-party preparations which she had been obsessed with from early in the morning, immediately after my father had left the house my mother began her (to us long familiar) birthday-party frenzy with all the hysteria imaginable, and while she was chasing me and my sister up and down the stairs and into the cellar and into the various outbuildings, in and out and back again, ceaselessly anxious not to make a mistake, chasing my sister and me around the entire house, hither and thither, with her birthday-party preparations, I was thinking all the time, I remember this quite clearly, is this now our father's fifty-eighth or is it the fifty-ninth birthday? all the time I ran around the house and around all the rooms thinking: is it the fifty-eighth or is it the fifty-ninth, or is it possibly the sixtieth? which in the end it was not, it was my father's fifty-ninth birthday, Reger said. I had been instructed to open all the windows and let in the fresh air, even then, in my childhood and youth, I hated a draught, but at the command of our mother I had to open all the windows at every other moment and to let in the air, he said, I therefore always had to do something I hated and I hated nothing more than letting fresh air into the house through all the windows,

I hated nothing more than the *draught* rushing into the house from all sides, he said, but naturally I could not do anything against the parental commands, I always meticulously executed all parental commands, I would never have dared not to execute a parental command, no matter whether it was a maternal or a paternal command, I automatically executed my parental command meticulously, Reger said, because I wished to escape parental punishment and that parental punishment was always dreadful and cruel, I feared parental torture and so I naturally always executed all parental commands meticulously, he said, no matter what the command was, even when in my opinion it was the most nonsensical of commands, it was therefore a matter of course that I opened all the windows on that birthday of my father and let the draught blow into the house. Our mother celebrated all our birthdays, not a single one of our birthdays was not celebrated, I hated those birthday celebrations, as you may imagine, just as I hate any celebrations, I hate anything festive, anything solemn to this day, nothing is more distasteful to me than celebrating or being celebrated, I am a hater of festivities, he said, from childhood I have hated all feasting and celebrating and above all I have hated birthday celebrations, no matter what birthday it was, and most of all I hated a parental birthday being celebrated; how can a person celebrate a birthday, his birthday, I have always wondered, when it is a misfortune to be in this world at all; yes, I always thought if people were to observe a memorial hour on their birthday, a memorial hour *for the monstrous deed their progenitors had committed against them*, that I would understand, but surely not a festivity, he said. And our father's birthdays were celebrated with all kinds of revolting pomp, all sorts of people I hated were invariably invited, and there was a lot of eating and drinking, and the most detestable thing of course were the speeches addressed to the person celebrated and the presents given to the person celebrated. Surely there is nothing more false than these birthday celebrations to which people lend themselves, nothing more distasteful than those birthday lies and those birthday hypocrisies, he said. It was in fact on our father's fifty-ninth birthday that my sister died, Reger said. I was standing in a corner on the first floor and, while trying to shield myself against the cold draught of air, was watching my mother rushing about the place with birthday-hysterical rapidity, at one moment transporting a vase from one room to another, at another switching a sugar bowl from one table to another table, one doily this way, another doily another way, a book to one place, another book to another place, a bunch of flowers over here, another over there, when suddenly, coming from downstairs, from the ground floor, I heard a dull thud, Reger said. My mother had stopped, because she too had heard the dull thud from downstairs. My mother stood still on the spot and her face had turned pale, Reger said. Something terrible had happened, that was instantly obvious to me as it was to my mother. I went down from the first floor to the vestibule and found my sister lying dead in the vestibule. Ah yes, Reger said, instant heart failure is an enviable death. If only we ourselves had such an instant heart failure one day, that would be the greatest happiness, he said. We hope for a swift painless death and yet we can drift into prolonged, year-long lingering illness, Reger said yesterday, adding that it was a consolation to him that his wife did not suffer long, not for years as sometimes happens, he said, only a few weeks. But of course there is no consolation for the loss of the one person who, all one's life, has been the closest to you. One method, he said yesterday, while I was now, that is a day later, observing him from the side, with Irrsigler behind him who had for one moment looked into the Sebastiano Room without taking any notice of me, while I was therefore still observing Reger who was still observing Tintoretto's *White-Bearded Man*, one method, he said, is to turn everything into a caricature. We can only stand a great, important picture if we have turned it into a caricature, or a great man, a so-called important personality, neither can we bear a person as a great man or as an important personality, he said, we have to caricature him. When we observe a picture for any length of time, even the most serious picture, we have to turn it into a caricature in order to bear it, hence we must also turn our parents, our superiors, if we have any, into caricatures, and the whole world into a caricature, he said. Look upon one of Rembrandt's self-portraits for any length of time, no matter which of them, in time it will quite certainly turn into a caricature for you and you will turn away. Look for any length of time at your father's face and it will turn into a caricature for you and you will turn away from him. Read Kant *intently and ever more intently* and you will suddenly be seized by a fit of laughter, he said. Strictly speaking, every original is a forgery in itself, he said. You follow my meaning. Of course there are phenomena in the world, in nature, if you like, which we *cannot* make look ridiculous, but in art *anything* can be made to look *ridiculous*, any person can be made to look ridiculous, can be made into a caricature whenever we like, whenever we feel the need, he said. Provided we are in a position to make something look ridiculous. We are not always in that position, and then we are seized by despair and next by the devil, he said. No matter which work of art, it can be made to look ridiculous, he said, it seems to you great and yet from one moment to the next you make it seem ridiculous, just as a person whom you have to make to look ridiculous because you cannot do otherwise. But then most people *are* ridiculous and most works of art *are* ridiculous, Reger said, and you can save yourself the trouble of making them look ridiculous or caricaturing them. Most people, on the other hand, are incapable of caricaturing, they observe everything to the bitter end with their terrible seriousness, he said, it never even occurs to them to caricature them, he said. You go to an audience of the Pope, he said, and you take the Pope and the audience seriously, moreover for the rest of your life; ridiculous, the history of the papacy is full of nothing but caricatures, he said. Of course, Saint Peter's is great, he said, but it is still ridiculous. Just step into Saint Peter's and free yourself completely of those hundreds and thousands and millions of Catholic lies about history, you do not have to wait long before the whole of Saint Peter's seems ridiculous to you. Go to a private audience and wait for the Pope, even before he arrives he will seem ridiculous to you, and of course he is ridiculous when he enters in his kitschy white pure silk robes. You can look around wherever you like, everything in the Vatican is ridiculous once you have freed yourself of the Catholic lies about history and of the

Catholic sentimentality about history, of the Catholic officiousness about world history. Think of it, the Catholic Pope as a shrewd globetrotting puppet, wearing make-up, sitting under his bullet-proof glass dome, surrounded by his make-up-wearing and shrewd super-puppets and under-puppets, how revoltingly ridiculous. Talk to one of our last and still-lamented kings, how ridiculous, talk to one of our blinkered communist leaders, how ridiculous. Go to the New Year's reception of our garrulous Federal President who, with his senile father-of-the-state babbling, makes a hash of everything he talks about, it is ridiculous enough to make you sick. The Capuchin Tomb, the *Hofburg*, what revolting ridiculousness. Go to the Maltese Church and look at those Maltese Knights in their black Maltese robes and their white pseudo-aristocratic numskulls glistening under the church lamps, and you will feel nothing except its ridiculousness. Go to a lecture by the Catholic cardinal, attend an inauguration at the university, how ridiculous. Wherever we look today in this country, we look into a sump of ridiculousness, Reger said. Every morning we blush at so much ridiculousness, my dear Atzbacher, that is the truth. Go to the presentation of a prize, Atzbacher, how ridiculous; ridiculous figures; the more bombastically they act the more ridiculous they are, he said, nothing but caricature, he said, simply everything. You call a good man your friend, and the next thing you know he lets himself be made an honorary professor and from then on calls himself professor and has *Professor* printed on his notepaper and his wife suddenly turns up at her butcher's as *Frau Professor* so she does not have to queue as long as the others who are not married to professors. How ridiculous, he said. Golden staircases, golden chairs, golden settees in the *Hofburg*, he said, and nothing but pseudo-democratic idiots on them, how ridiculous. You walk down Kärntnerstrasse and everything seems to you ridiculous, all the people are just ridiculous, nothing else. You walk right across Vienna, this way and that, and all Vienna seems suddenly ridiculous to you, all the people coming towards you are ridiculous people, everything that comes towards you is ridiculous, you live in an utterly ridiculous and in reality debased world. You suddenly have to turn the whole world into a caricature. You have the strength to turn the world into a caricature, he said, the supreme strength of the spirit which is necessary for it, this one strength for survival, he said. We only control what we ultimately find ridiculous, only if we find the world and life upon it ridiculous can we get any further, there is no other, no better, method, he said. We cannot endure a state of admiration for long, and we perish if we do not break it off in time, he said. I have all my life been far from being an admirer, admiration is alien to me, as there are no miracles admiration has always been alien to me and nothing repels me more than observing people in the act of admiration, people infected with some admiration. You enter a church and the people there admire, you enter a museum and the people admire. You go to a concert and the people admire, that is distasteful. Real intellect does not know admiration: it acknowledges, it respects, it esteems, that is all, he said. People enter every church and every museum as though with a rucksack full of admiration, and for that reason they always have that revolting stooping way of walking which they all have in churches and in museums, he said. I have never yet seen a person enter a church or a museum entirely normally, and the most distasteful thing is to watch those people in Knossos or in Agrigento, when they have arrived at the destination of their admiration journey, because the journeys these people undertake are nothing but admiration journeys, he said. Admiration makes a person blind, Reger said yesterday, it makes the admirers dull-witted. Most people, once they have got into admiration never get out of admiration again, and that makes them dull-witted. Most people are dull-witted all their lives solely because they keep admiring. There is nothing to admire, Reger said yesterday, nothing, nothing at all. But because people find respect and esteem too difficult for them they admire, that comes cheaper for them, Reger said. Admiration is easier than respect, admiration is the characteristic of the dimwit, Reger said. Only a dimwit admires, the intelligent person does not admire but respects, esteems, understands, that is it. But respect and esteem and understanding require a mind, and a mind is what people do not have, without a mind and in fact totally mindlessly they travel to the pyramids and to the Sicilian columns and to the Persian temples and sprinkle themselves and their dull-wittedness with admiration, he said. The state of admiration is a state of feeble-mindedness, Reger said yesterday, nearly all of them live in this state of feeble-mindedness. And in that state of feeble-mindedness they all enter the Kunsthistorisches Museum, he said. The people are weighed down by their admiration, they do not have the courage to deposit their admiration in the cloakroom along with their overcoats. So they drag themselves, laboriously crammed full of admiration, through all these rooms, Reger said, so much so it turns your stomach. Admiration, however, is not just the characteristic of the so-called uneducated, quite the opposite, it is also to a quite frightful, yes, literally a frightening degree, a characteristic of the so-called educated, which is a lot more revolting still.

The uneducated person admires because quite simply he is too stupid not to admire; the educated person, however, is actually perverse, Reger said. The admiration of the so-called uneducated is entirely natural, the admiration of the so-called educated, on the other hand, is a positively perverse perverseness, Reger said. Take Beethoven, the permanently depressive, the state artist, the total state composer: the people admire him, but basically Beethoven is an utterly repulsive phenomenon, everything about Beethoven is more or less comical, a comical helplessness is what we continually hear when we are listening to Beethoven: the rancour, the titanic, the marching-tune dull-wittedness even in his chamber music. When we hear Beethoven's music we hear more noise than music, the state-dulled march of the notes, Reger said. I listen to Beethoven for a time, for instance to the *Eroica*, and I listen, attentively and I actually get into a philosophical-mathematical state and I remain in a philosophical-mathematical state for a long time, Reger said, until all of a sudden I *see* the creator of the *Eroica* and everything is spoiled for me, because *in Beethoven everything is really marching*, I listen to the *Eroica*, which is in fact philosophical music, thoroughly philosophical and mathematical music, Reger said, and suddenly it is all spoiled for me and ruined because, while the Philharmonic play it in such a matter-of-fact way, I hear Beethoven's failure from one moment to the next, *hear* his failure, *see* his march-music head, you know what I mean, Reger said. Beethoven by then has become unbearable to me, just as I find it unbearable when I hear one of our big-bellied or thin-bellied singers kill the *Winterreise* with his singing, you understand, because that lieder-singing singer wearing tails and resting his hand on the piano while singing *The Crow* is always unbearable to me and ridiculous, he is a caricature from the outset, there is nothing more ridiculous, Reger said, than a lieder- or aria-singing singer leaning against the grand piano in tails. How magnificent is Schubert's music when we do not see it being performed, when we do not see those abysmally dull-witted conceited curly-haired interpreters, but we do, of course, see them when we are in the concert hall and everything as a result becomes embarrassing and ridiculous and an acoustic and visual disaster. I do not know, Reger said, if the pianists are more ridiculous and more embarrassing than the singers by the piano, it is a question of the state of mind we happen to be in at the moment. Of course anything we see while music is being performed is ridiculous, a caricature, and therefore embarrassing, he said. The singer is ridiculous and embarrassing, he may sing as he will, no matter whether tenor or bass, and all women singers are invariably even more ridiculous and embarrassing, no matter how they are gowned or what they sing, he said. A person bowing or plucking on the podium – it is too ridiculous, he said. Even the *obese smelly* Bach at the organ of Saint Thomas's Church was only a ridiculous and deeply embarrassing figure, there can be no argument about that. No, no, all artists, even if they are the most important ones and, as it were, the greatest, are nothing, except kitschy and embarrassing and ridiculous. Toscanini, Furtwängler, the one too small and the other too tall, ridiculous and kitschy. And if you go to the theatre the ridiculousness and the embarrassment and the kitsch make you feel positively sick. No matter what or how the people speak, they make you feel sick. If they speak classical parts they make you feel sick, if they speak popular parts they make you feel sick. And what else are all those classical and modern so-called high or popular dramas but theatrical ridiculousness and kitschy embarrassment, he said. The whole world today is ridiculous and at the same time profoundly embarrassing and kitschy, that is the truth. Irrsigler was stepping up to Reger and once more whispering something in his ear. Reger stood up, looked about himself and left the Bordone Room with Irrsigler. I glanced at my watch, there were ten minutes to go to half-past eleven. One reason why I had come to the museum as early as half-past ten was to be absolutely punctual, for Reger demanded nothing more than punctuality, just as I myself always demand punctuality more than anything else, in fact punctuality to me is the most important thing in dealing with people. I can only bear the punctual ones, I cannot bear an unpunctual person. Punctuality is an essential characteristic of Reger just as it is one of my essential characteristics, when I have an appointment I keep it *strictly punctually*, just as Reger keeps all his appointments punctually, he has given me numerous lectures on punctuality, just as he has on reliability; punctuality and reliability are the most important aspects of a person, Reger has very frequently said to me. I may say that I am a thoroughly punctual person, I have always hated unpunctuality and besides I have never been able to afford it. Reger is the most punctual person I know. He has *never in his whole life been late, at least not through his own fault*, as he says, just as I have never in my whole life been late, at least not in my adult life, through my own fault, unpunctual people to me are the most hateful people, I have nothing in common with unpunctual people, I do not keep up with un-punctual people, I have nothing to do with unpunctual people and I do not wish to have anything to do with them. Unpunctuality is a characteristic of gross negligence, which I despise and detest, which brings nothing but demoralization and misfortune to people. *Unpunctuality is a disease which leads to the death of the unpunctual*, Reger once said to me. Reger had got up and left the Bordone Room just as a group of elderly men, Russians as I was immediately able to establish, was entering the Bordone Room, led, as I likewise established just as quickly, by a Ukrainian woman interpreter, and passed me, moreover passed me in such a way that they forced me aside and into the corner. People will crowd into a room, pushing a person aside without even apologizing, I reflected, and already I found myself pushed against the wall. Reger had left the Bordone Room after Irrsigler had whispered something in his ear and at just that moment the Russian group had entered the Bordone Room and taken up position in the Bordone Room, entering the Bordone Room and taking up position in the Bordone Room in such a way that I was no longer able to look into the Bordone Room from the Sebastiano Room; the Russian group had totally blocked my view of the Bordone Room. I only saw the backs of the Russian group and heard what the Ukrainian interpreter had to offer to them, like all other guides in the Kunsthistorisches Museum she was talking nonsense, it was nothing but the usual sickening art twaddle that she stuffed into the heads of her Russian victims. *Look at this*, she said, *look at this mouth, and here,* she said, *look at these projecting ears, and here, look at this delicate pink on the angel's cheek, and here in the background you can see the horizon,* as if everybody could not see all these things in the Tintoretto paintings without those inane remarks. Museum guides invariably treat their charges as dimwits, invariably as the worst dimwits, whereas in fact they never are such dimwits, they explain to them chiefly those things which can, of course, be seen perfectly clearly and therefore do not need to be explained, yet they explain and explain and point and point and talk and talk. The museum guides are nothing but conceited twaddling machines, switched on for the duration of a group's tour through the museum, such twaddling machines utter the same words year after year. The museum guides are nothing but conceited art twaddlers who do not have the faintest idea about art but unscrupulously exploit art with their distasteful twaddle. The museum guides rattle off their art twaddle all year long and collect a pile of money for it. I had been pushed into the corner by the Russian group and saw nothing but those Russian backs, that is to say nothing but heavy Russian winter coats, all of them exuding a penetrating smell of naphthalene, since the Russian group had evidently had to make their way straight from their bus to the picture gallery in a drizzle. As I have suffered from respiratory problems for many decades and in any case feel, several times a day, that I am *about to choke*, even out of doors, those moments, which in fact were minutes, behind the Russian group were repulsive to me, pressed against the wall of the Bordone Room I was all the time inhaling air reeking of naphthalene, air much too heavy for my weak lungs. After all, I find it difficult enough to breathe in the Kunsthistorisches Museum, let alone under such conditions as the arrival of the Russian group. The Ukrainian guide talked to the Russian group in what is known as classical Muscovite Russian and I understood most of it, but she had a terrible, positively painful, pronunciation if she said anything in German, the *way* she said the word *Engelskopf* was quite ghastly. I was unable at first to say whether the interpreter had come from Russia with the Russian group or whether she was one of those Russian *émigrées* who had come to Vienna after the war and who are still coming to Vienna, those Russian Jewish *émigrée* women who are highly intelligent and who have always set the fashion behind the scenes in Vienna, which has invariably been of advantage to Viennese intellectual society. These Russian Jewish *émigrée* women are the real intellectual seasoning of Viennese society life, they have always been just that, without them Viennese intellectual life would be uninteresting. Admittedly these people, if, as it were, they turn megalomaniac and try to dominate absolutely everything, also soon get on your nerves, but then this woman interpreter was not exactly a prime example of the kind of Russian women *émigrées* I have in mind, if indeed she was such a Russian *émigrée;* she looked to me more as if she had come to Vienna from Russia with her Russian group, the way she spoke to the Russian group in *their Russian* argued against the assumption that she was a Russian *émigrée* and in favour of her having come to Vienna with the Russian group, and quite possibly arrived in Vienna from Russia only that very day, at least that is what I immediately thought when I had taken a closer look at her clothes, in particular her boots, there was in fact nothing Western about her, she probably was a communist who had been trained as an art historian, I thought as I scrutinized her from head to toe, as it were, the moment I had an opportunity to do so. The Russian women *émigrées* I have mentioned, after all, dress in a predominantly Western manner, albeit not *as* Western as real Westerners, but in a Western manner all the same. No, that interpreter is not a Russian *émigrée*, I thought, she crossed the frontier with the Russian group last night and did not even sleep last night, any more than the Russian group in her charge, the group has come to the museum straight from Russia, as it were, and straight from their dirty bus, I thought, that's what she looked like, that's what the woman interpreter looked like, that's what the group looked like. Because the Russian group was blocking my view I could not now see the velvet settee in the Bordone Room, I could not therefore see whether Reger was still outside or whether he had meanwhile returned to the room. The Sebastiano Room, where I was standing pressed against the wall, is the worst ventilated room in the Kunsthistorisches Museum, and of all places, I reflected, I had to be pushed against the wall by the Russian group in the Sebastiano Room, and of all people, I reflected, by such a crowd smelling of garlic and mud and dampness. I have always detested crowds, I have avoided them all my life, I have never gone to any meeting, no matter what, because of my detestation of crowds, just as Reger, incidentally, had not either, I hate nothing more profoundly than the multitude, than a crowd, I continually believe, even without seeking them out, that I am going to be crushed by the multitude or by the crowd. Even as a child I avoided multitudes, I detested crowds, the accumulation of people, the concentration of vileness and mindlessness and lies. Much as we *should* love each individual, I believe, so we hate the mass. Of course this Russian group was not the first I had encountered at the Kunsthistorisches Museum or that, as it were, assaulted me at the

Kunsthistorisches Museum and pushed me against the wall, Russian groups have lately been coming to the Kunsthistorisches Museum in greater numbers, indeed it seems as if there are now more Russian groups at the Kunsthistorisches Museum than Italian ones. The Russians and the Italians always appear at the Kunsthistorisches Museum in groups, whereas the English never appear in groups but always on their own, the French likewise always appear on their own. There are days when the Russian guides, men and women, have a shouting match with the Italians and the Kunsthistorisches Museum becomes a shouting house. That, of course, mostly happens on Saturdays, that is on a day when Reger and I *never* go to the Kunsthistorisches Museum; that Reger and I have come to the Kunsthistorisches Museum today, on a Saturday, is an exception to the rule and, as can be seen, we have done well not to go to the Kunsthistorisches Museum on a Saturday, even though admission on Saturdays is free, as it is also on Sundays. I would sooner pay those twenty schillings for a ticket, Reger said to me once, than be exposed to those ghastly groups. Exposing oneself to groups of museum visitors is a punishment of heaven, I cannot think of anything more terrible, Reger said to me once. No doubt it was a punishment of heaven for him, albeit a self-invited one, that he made an appointment with me at the Kunsthistorisches

Museum on this Saturday of all days, I thought, wondering about his purpose and unable to answer my question. Needless to say I should also have liked to know what it was Irrsigler had whispered in his ear, the first time it was something which evidently did not concern him in the least, and the second time it was something which made Reger immediately get up from the settee in the Bordone Room and walk out of the Bordone Room. Irrsigler misses no opportunity to point out that his is a *position of trust*, it is touching the way he says it, and he says it so often that it becomes more touching with each repetition. Irrsigler nods his head when Reger arrives and he spots him, he does not do so when he sees *me*. Three times already Irrsigler has received a loan from Reger for the purpose of furnishing his flat, a loan over several years, which he did not in the end have to repay to Reger. Reger had repeatedly made Irrsigler presents of clothes he no longer wears, truly top-quality treasures from the most superb tweed material; as Reger once said to me: *everything I wear comes from the Hebrides*. But Irrsigler gets little opportunity to wear Reger's sartorial treasures because all week long he is on duty in his uniform at the Kunsthistorisches Museum, except Mondays, but on Monday he is at home in his dungarees because his Mondays are invariably taken up with domestic jobs. He does everything himself. He does his own painting, he does his own carpentry, he nails and drills and even welds everything himself. Eighty per cent of all Austrians spend their leisure time in dungarees, Reger maintains, and most of them even on Sundays and holidays, the majority of all Austrians walk around in working clothes on Sundays and holidays, painting and nailing and welding. An Austrian's leisure hours are his real working hours, Reger maintains. Most Austrians do not know what to do with their leisure time and so they will kill it dull-wittedly. All week long they sit in their offices or stand at their workplaces, Reger says, and invariably on Sundays and holidays one can see them, without exception, slipping on their dungarees and performing jobs at home, they paint their own four walls or hammer nails into their roofs or wash their cars. Irrsigler, Reger says, is such a typical Austrian, and the Burgenlanders are the most typical Austrians anyway. A Burgenlander gets into his Sunday best for only two, or at the most three hours once a week to go to church, the rest of the time he wears his dungarees, which are his working clothes, and this he will do as long as he lives, Reger says. A Burgenlander works all the week in his dungarees, he sleeps strikingly little but well, and on Sundays and holy days he goes to church in his Sunday best to sing a hymn to the Lord, only to slip out of his Sunday best and back into his dungarees immediately afterwards. A Burgenlander is still a typical peasant even in today's industrial society, even if a Burgenlander has worked in a factory for a number of decades he still remains the peasant his ancestors were, a Burgenlander will always be a peasant, Reger says. Irrsigler has lived in Vienna for a great many years and yet he has remained a peasant, Reger said. A peasant, incidentally, has always been comfortable in uniform, Reger said. A peasant either remains a peasant or he slips on a uniform, Reger said. If there are several children one will remain a peasant and the rest will slip on a state uniform or the Christian Catholic uniform, this is how it has always been, Reger said. A Burgenlander is either a peasant or he slips on a uniform; if he cannot be a peasant or slip on a uniform he inevitably comes to grief, Reger said. The peasantry, when it wished to escape from peasantry, has always, for centuries, escaped into a uniform, Reger said. Irrsigler, he believed, had been lucky because posts as state-employed attendants at the Kunsthistorisches Museum only come up every few years, in fact only when one of the attendants leaves or dies. Burgenlanders were favoured for employment as museum attendants – why, that he, Irrsigler, could not say, but it was a fact that the majority of museum attendants in Vienna were Burgenlanders. Probably, Irrsigler suggested on one occasion, because

Burgenlanders were regarded as particularly honest but also as particularly stupid and undemanding. Because they, the Burgenlanders, even today still had an *intact character*. When he considered what things were like in the police, then he was glad the police had not accepted him. He also mentioned that at one time he had had an idea of entering a monastery, because there too a person's clothes were provided, and the monasteries were nowadays looking for replacements as never before; however, as a *lay brother* in a monastery he would *only have been exploited by those in superior positions*, as he expressed himself, *by the priests who made a rather pleasant life for themselves in the monasteries at the expense of the lay brothers who were totally subject to them*. All he would have done there, he said, was *chop wood and feed the pigs* and in summer thin out the cabbages and in winter shovel the monastery paths clear of snow. The lay brothers in the monasteries are poor worms, Irrsigler once said, he did not wish to be a poor worm. Although his parents would have been pleased to see him enter a monastery; *I could have entered at once*, he said, he had actually been on the point of entering one in the Tyrol. To be a lay brother was even worse than being a convict in a penal institution, Irrsigler said. *The monks in holy orders had it made for them*, he said, *but the lay brothers* were *nothing but slaves*. In the monasteries, he said, medieval slavery still existed as far as the lay brothers were concerned, it was no joke being a lay brother and at mealtimes all they got were the left-overs. He had had no wish to be a servant to pot-bellied theologians, to what Reger called *abusers of God*, who enjoyed a life of plenty in the monasteries, he had said *no* at the right moment. On one occasion Reger had gone to the Prater with the Irrsigler family, Reger's wife by then had been very ill. Contact with children always bothered him, Reger said, he had always only been able to stand children for a very short time, he had not to be in the middle of a *work process* when meeting children, it had been an adventure inviting the Irrsigler family to a visit to the Prater but he, Reger, had for some time felt that he owed something to Irrsigler, *because in actual fact I make use at the Kunsthistorisches Museum of something I am not entitled to, I sit for hours on the settee in the Bordone Room*, Reger said, *in order to think, in order to reflect and even in order to read books and essays, I sit on the Bordone Room settee which is provided there for normal visitors to the museum, not for me, and quite certainly not for me over a period of thirty years*, Reger said. I expect Irrsigler to let me sit on the Bordone Room settee every other day without being entitled to expect this, after all quite often other people in the Bordone Room would like to sit down on the Bordone Room settee but cannot do so because

I am sitting on the Bordone Room settee, Reger said. By now the Bordone Room settee has more or less become a prerequisite of my thinking, Reger again said to me yesterday, the Bordone Room settee suits me much better than the Ambassador, where I also have an ideal seat for thinking, on the Bordone Room settee I think with a much greater intensity than I do at the Ambassador, where I also think since I never discontinue my thinking, Reger said, as you know *I think all the time*, indeed I also think in my sleep, but on the Bordone Room settee I think the way I have to think, therefore I sit on the Bordone Room settee for thinking. Every other day I sit on the Bordone Room settee, Reger said, naturally not every day, for that really would be destructive, I mean if I sat on the Bordone Room settee every day, that would destroy everything within me that I value, and nothing of course is more valuable to me than thinking, I think therefore I live, I live therefore I think, Reger said, I therefore sit on the Bordone Room settee every other day and remain sitting there on the Bordone Room settee for at least three or four hours, which of course means no less then than that I occupy the Bordone Room settee for those three or four, sometimes five, hours for my exclusive use and no one else can sit on the Bordone Room settee. For the exhausted visitors to the museum, who enter the Bordone Room totally exhausted and would like to sit down on the Bordone Room settee, it is of course unfortunate that I am sitting on the Bordone Room settee but I cannot do otherwise, even as I wake up at home I already think about sitting on the Bordone Room settee as soon as possible in order not to fall prey to despair; if ever I were unable to sit on the Bordone Room settee I should be in the depths of despair, Reger said. Throughout these more than thirty years Irrsigler has always kept the Bordone Room settee for me, Reger said, only once did I come to the Bordone Room and found the Bordone Room settee occupied, an Englishman in plus-fours had sat down on the Bordone Room settee and was not to be induced to get up from the Bordone Room settee, not even in response to Irrsigler's insistent pleas, not even in response to my pleas, it was all no use, the Englishman remained seated on the Bordone Room settee, Reger said, and took no notice either of me or of Irrsigler. He had come specially from England, or more correctly from Wales, to the Kunsthistorisches Museum in Vienna in order to look at the *White-Bearded Man*, the Englishman from Wales said, according to Reger, and he could see no reason why he should get up from the settee which was surely intended for visitors to the museum who were particularly interested in Tintoretto's *White-Bearded Man*. I had argued with the Englishman for some time, but the Englishman eventually no longer listened, he was therefore no longer interested in what I was saying in order to make him understand how important sitting on the Bordone Room settee was for me, what significance the Bordone Room settee had for me. Irrsigler had told the Englishman, who incidentally was wearing a high-quality Scottish jacket, Reger said, that the settee on which he was sitting was reserved for me, which of course was totally contrary to regulations since not a single settee in the Kunsthistorisches Museum can ever be a reserved settee, by this remark Irrsigler had placed himself in the wrong, Reger said, but he actually said the settee was reserved; the Englishman, however, had taken no notice either of what Irrsigler had said to him nor of what I had said to him with regard to the Bordone Room settee, he had calmly let us speak while making notes on a little notepad, presumably, as I assumed, relating to the *White-Bearded Man*. The Englishman from Wales might *possibly be an interesting person*, I thought, Reger said, and I thought that rather than engaging on my feet in a by then pointless and useless argument about the Bordone Room settee, whose importance to me I should have never been able to make him understand, I would simply sit down on the settee next to the Englishman from Wales, and so, needless to say, in all politeness I quite simply sat

down on the settee next to him. The Englishman from
Wales moved a few centimetres over to the right so
that I could sit down on the left. I had never before
sat on the Bordone Room settee *à deux*, as it were,
this was the first time. Irrsigler was obviously relieved
that by sitting down on the Bordone Room settee I had
defused the situation and he presently disappeared in
response to a brief signal from me, Reger said, while
I, just as the Englishman from Wales, once more
inspected the *White-Bearded Man*. Are you really
interested in the *White-Bearded Man*? I asked the
Englishman and received, as a kind of delayed
response, a short nod of his English head. My question
had been nonsensical and I instantly regretted having
put it; I thought, Reger said, I have just asked one of
the stupidest questions that could be asked, and I
decided to say no more and to wait in complete
silence for the Englishman to get up and leave. But
the Englishman had no intention of getting up and
leaving, on the contrary he took out of his jacket
pocket a thicker book, bound in black leather and read
something in it; he alternately read his book and
looked up at the *White-Bearded Man*, while I had
noticed that he used *Aqua brava*, a toilet water that I
find by no means unpleasant. If that Englishman uses
Aqua brava, I thought, he has good taste. People who
use *Aqua brava* all have good taste, an Englishman,

moreover an Englishman from Wales, who uses *Aqua brava* is therefore not unlikeable to me, I thought, Reger said. Now and again Irrsigler appeared on the scene to see whether the Englishman had by then disappeared, Reger said, but the Englishman had no intention of disappearing, he would read several pages of his black leather book and then for several minutes study the *White-Bearded Man* and the other way about, and it looked as if he intended *to remain seated on the Bordone Room settee for a very long time.* Anything they tackle the English tackle thoroughly, just as the Germans, whenever art is concerned, Reger said, and in all my life I had never seen a more thorough Englishman where art was concerned. No doubt the man sitting next to me was a so-called art expert and I thought, Reger said, you have always hated art experts and now you are sitting next to such an art expert and actually find him likeable, not only because he uses *Aqua brava*, not only because of his high-quality Scottish clothes, but gradually likeable generally, Reger said. Anyway, Reger said, the Englishman read his black leather book for at least half an hour or more and just as long looked at Tintoretto's *White-Bearded Man*, in other words he sat next to me on the Bordone Room settee for a whole hour, until he abruptly got up, turned to me and asked what I was actually doing there in the Bordone Room, surely it was most unusual for someone to sit more than an hour in a room such as the Bordone Room, *on this exceedingly uncomfortable settee*, staring at the *White-Bearded Man*. Needless to say, I was completely taken aback, Reger said, and did not know at the moment how to reply to the Englishman. Well, I said, I did not know myself what I was doing here, I said to the Englishman from Wales, I could not think of anything else to say. The Englishman looked at me with irritation, just as if he regarded me as an absolute fool, *Bordone*, the Englishman said, *unimportant; Tintoretto, well yes*, he said. The Englishman took a handkerchief from his left trouser pocket and put it in his right one. A typical gesture of embarrassment, I said to myself, and as the Englishman, whom I had suddenly begun to like, was about to leave, having long pocketed his black leather book and his notepad, I invited him to sit down again on the Bordone Room settee and keep me company for a little while, he interested me, I told him frankly, there was a certain fascination for me about him, I told him, Reger said to me. Thus for the first time I made the acquaintance of an Englishman from Wales who seemed absolutely likeable to me, Reger said, because generally speaking I do not find the English likeable, just as, incidentally, I do not the French either, nor the Poles, nor the Russians, not to mention the Scandinavians whom I have never found likeable. A

likeable Englishman is a curiosity, I said to myself
when I had sat down again with him, having of course
stood up as the Englishman stood up. I was interested
to know whether the Englishman had really come to
the Kunsthistorisches Museum solely for the *White-
Bearded Man*, Reger said, and I therefore asked him if
that was really his reason, and the Englishman nodded
his head. Incidentally, he was speaking English, which
I found agreeable, but then suddenly also German,
very broken German, that broken German which
all Englishmen speak when they believe they know
German, which, however, is never the case, Reger said,
the Englishman probably wanted to speak German
rather than English in order to improve his German,
and after all why not, when abroad one prefers to
speak the foreign language unless one is a blockhead,
and so in his broken German he said that he had in
fact come to Austria and to Vienna solely for the
White-Bearded Man, not because of Tintoretto, he said,
Reger said, but solely for the *White-Bearded Man*, he
was not interested in the museum as a whole, not in
the least, he was not one for museums, he hated
museums and had always only visited them reluctantly,
he had only come to the Vienna Kunsthistorisches
Museum in order to study the *White-Bearded Man*
because *back home he had just such a White-Bearded
Man* hanging over his bed in his bedroom in Wales,

in actual fact the same White-Bearded Man, the English-man said, Reger said. I was told, the Englishman said, that at the Vienna Kunsthistorisches Museum there was just such a *White-Bearded Man* as in my bedroom in Wales and that has been worrying me and so I have come to Vienna. For two years I had been worrying in my bedroom in Wales at the thought that just such a *White-Bearded Man* by Tintoretto was possibly really hanging at the Kunsthistorisches Museum in Vienna as in my bedroom, and so I travelled to Vienna yesterday. Believe it or not, the Englishman said, Reger said to me, the same *White-Bearded Man* by Tintoretto which hangs in my bedroom in Wales also hangs here. I could not believe my eyes, the Englishman said, naturally in English, and when I assured myself that this *White-Bearded Man* is the same as the one in my bedroom I was at first profoundly shocked. You concealed your shock very well, I said to the English-man, Reger said to me. But then the English have always been masters of self-control, I said to the Englishman from Wales, Reger said, even at moments of extreme excitement they preserve their calm and sang-froid, I said to the Englishman, Reger said to me. All this time I compared my *White-Bearded Man* by Tintoretto, the one hanging in my bedroom in Wales, with the *White-Bearded Man* by Tintoretto in this room, the Englishman said and, producing his black leather book from his pocket, showed me in it a reproduction of *his* Tintoretto. Yes, indeed, I said to the Englishman, the Tintoretto reproduced in the book is the same as the one hanging here on the wall. You see, the Englishman from Wales said, you say so too! It is the same picture down to the last detail, I said, Tintoretto's *White-Bearded Man* in your book is the same as the one hanging here on the wall. Right down to the last detail, as the phrase goes, you are bound to say that everything matches in the most startling manner, as if it were really one and the same picture, I said, Reger said to me. Yet the Englishman was not at all excited, Reger said, I would not have remained so cool in the face of the fact that the picture in the Bordone Room is in fact identical with the picture in my bedroom, Reger said, the Englishman looked at his black leather book in which the *White-Bearded Man* from his bedroom in Wales was reproduced on a whole page and, as the phrase goes, in full colour, and again at the *White-Bearded Man* in the Bordone Room. A nephew of mine was in Vienna two years ago and because he did not want to go to concerts every day he went to the Kunsthistorisches Museum one Tuesday, without actually being really interested, the Englishman said, Reger said, one of my numerous nephews who make a major trip every year to Europe or America or Asia, or wherever, and

there, at the Kunsthistorisches Museum, he saw
Tintoretto's *White-Bearded Man* hanging on the wall;
all excited he came to see me and told me he had,
in a manner of speaking, seen *my Tintoretto at the
Kunsthistorisches Museum*. Naturally I did not believe
his story and laughed at my nephew, the Englishman
said, Reger said, I regarded the whole business as a
silly prank, one of those silly pranks my nephews
delight in playing on me all the time. *My Tintoretto in
Vienna at the Kunsthistorisches Museum?* I said, and I told
my nephew he was the victim of a delusion, he should
dismiss this absurdity from his mind. But my nephew
insisted: he had seen my Tintoretto hanging on the
wall at the Kunsthistorisches Museum in Vienna.
Naturally this unbelievable piece of information from
my nephew gnawed away at my mind and, basically,
gave me no peace. My nephew must be the victim
of some error, I kept thinking all along. But I could
not dismiss the business from my mind. Good Lord,
you cannot imagine the value of that Tintoretto, an
heirloom, a great-aunt on my mother's side, my
so-called Glasgow aunt, left me the Tintoretto, the
Englishman said, Reger said. I have the painting
hanging in my bedroom because there it seems safest
to me, there it hangs above my bed, *worst possible angle
for light*, the Englishman said, Reger said. Thousands
of old masters are stolen in England every day, the

Englishman said, Reger said, there are hundreds of organized gangs in England who specialize in the theft of old masters, especially of Italians, who are particularly popular in England. I am no art connoisseur, sir, the Englishman said, Reger said, I understand absolutely nothing about art, but of course I appreciate such a masterpiece. I could have sold it many times, but as yet I do not need to, not as yet, the Englishman said, Reger said, but of course the time may come when I have to sell the *White-Bearded Man*. I do not actually have only the *White-Bearded Man* by Tintoretto, I possess several dozen Italians, a Lotto, a Crespi, a Strozzi, a Giordano, a Bassano, all of them, you know, really great masters. All from the Glasgow aunt, the Englishman said, Reger said. I should have never come to Vienna if I had not been tormented by the suspicion that my nephew might after all be right when he says that my Tintoretto hangs at the Kunsthistorisches Museum in Vienna. I have never been interested in Vienna because I am not a music *connoisseur* either, not even a music *lover*, the Englishman said, Reger said, nothing would have made me come to Austria except that gnawing suspicion. And now I am sitting here and I see that my Tintoretto does in fact hang on the wall here at the Kunsthistorisches Museum. See for yourself, the *White- Bearded Man* in the reproduction here, the one that hangs in my bedroom in Wales, is the Tintoretto that hangs here on the wall at the Kunsthistorisches Museum, the Englishman said, Reger said, and once again the Englishman held open the black leather book before my eyes. It looks as if it is not merely the same but absolutely identical, the Englishman said, Reger said. The Englishman rose from the settee and stepped quite close to the *White-Bearded Man* and for a while remained standing in front of the *White-Bearded Man*. I observed the Englishman and admired him at the same time, because I had never yet seen a person with such positively super-human self-control, Reger said, I observed the Englishman from Wales and I reflected that, faced with such a monstrous situation, that is to say down to the last hair the very same picture hanging at the Kunsthistorisches Museum as in my bedroom in Wales, I would have completely lost my self-control. I watched the Englishman stepping up quite close to the *White-Bearded Man* and staring at him, naturally, as I was watching him from behind, I could not see his face, Reger said to me, but I knew of course, even though I was watching him from behind, that he was staring at the *White-Bearded Man*, now more or less disconcerted. For a long time the Englishman did not turn round, and when he did his face was as white as chalk, Reger said. I have rarely in my life seen a face quite as white as chalk, Reger said, least of all an

English face. Before rising from the settee and staring at the *White-Bearded Man*, the Englishman had *that typical red-tanned English face*, now his face was as white as chalk, Reger said about the Englishman. Disconcerted is not even an adequate expression, Reger said about the Englishman. Irrsigler had been watching the scene the whole time, Reger said, Irrsigler had silently stood in the corner which you pass to go to the Veronese paintings, Reger said. The Englishman sat down once more on the Bordone Room settee, on which I had remained sitting the whole time, and said that it was in fact *one and the same painting*, the one hanging over his bed in his bedroom in Wales and the one here on the wall of the Bordone Room at the Kunsthistorisches Museum. He was staying at the *Hotel Imperial*, which his nephew had recommended, the Englishman said, Reger said. I hate all that luxury but at the same time I enjoy it when I feel like it. He only ever stayed at the best hotels, the Englishman said, Reger said, *in Vienna of course at the Imperial, just as in Madrid at the Ritz, just as in Taormina at the Timeo.* But I greatly dislike travelling, only once every few years, and mostly the reason is not pleasure, the Englishman said, Reger said. It is perfectly obvious that one of these Tintoretto paintings is a forgery, the Englishman then said, Reger said, either this one here at the Kunsthistorisches Museum or mine, which hangs over my bed in my bedroom in Wales. *One of the two must be a forgery*, the Englishman said and briefly pressed his strong body against the backrest of the Bordone Room settee; at once, however, he straightened up and said, so my nephew was right after all. I cursed my nephew because I felt sure that he had told me some nonsense, because this nephew is in the habit of disquieting me from time to time with some business or other or perplexing me; incidentally, he is my favourite nephew even though he has got on my nerves as long as he has lived and is basically a good-for-nothing. But he is my favourite nephew. He is the most frightful of all my nephews but he is my favourite nephew. His eyes did not deceive him, the Englishman said, this Tintoretto here is in fact identical with mine in Wales. *But there are two Tintorettos*, the Englishman said then and once more leaned back on the Bordone Room settee only to straighten up again presently. One of the two is a forgery, he said, and of course I ask myself is mine a forgery or the one here at the Kunsthistorisches Museum? It is quite possible that the Kunsthistorisches Museum possesses a forgery and that my Tintoretto is genuine, indeed from what I know of the circumstances of my Glasgow aunt it is even probable. Shortly after Tintoretto painted this *White-Bearded Man*, the *White-Bearded Man* was sold to England, first to the family of the Duke of Kent, then to my Glasgow aunt. Incidentally, the brother of the present Duke of Kent is married to an Austrian, surely you know that, the Englishman suddenly said to me, Reger said, for the sake of a brief diversion, only to say immediately afterwards that the Tintoretto here, that is the *White-Bearded Man* at the Kunsthistorisches Museum, was quite certainly a forgery. *An absolutely perfect forgery*, the Englishman added. I shall discover very soon which *White- Bearded Man* by Tintoretto is the genuine and which the forgery, the Englishman said, Reger said, and then he said that it was also entirely possible that both *White-Bearded Men* might be genuine, that is by Tintoretto and genuine. Only a great artist like Tintoretto, the Englishman said, Reger said, could have succeeded in painting a second picture not *as a totally similar but as a totally identical one. That, of course, would be a sensation*, the Englishman said, Reger said, and walked out of the Bordone Room. He took leave of me with only a short *Goodbye*, and of Irrsigler, who had witnessed the whole scene, also with the same *goodbye*, Reger said to me. I do not know how the matter ended, Reger said, I have not concerned myself with it after that. Anyway, the Englishman was the person, Reger said, who was sitting on the Bordone Room settee on one occasion when I entered the Bordone Room. Apart from that, no one. Reger has had this illusion about the Bordone Room settee for more than thirty years, he maintains that he cannot think properly, that is *think in accordance with his head*, unless he is sitting on the Bordone Room settee. At the Ambassador I have some very good ideas, Reger keeps saying, but on the Bordone Room settee at the Kunsthistorisches Museum I have the best, unquestionably always the best ideas, while at the Ambassador it is scarcely possible to get any so-called philosophical thinking going, it is a matter of course on the Bordone Room settee. At the Ambassador I think the way everyone else thinks, everyday matters and everyday needs, but on the Bordone Room settee I think the unusual and the extraordinary. For instance, he would be unable at the Ambassador to explain the *Tempest Sonata* in the same concentrated manner as on the Bordone Room settee, and to give a lecture such as the one on the Art of the Fugue with all its profundity and all its particularities and peculiarities would be quite impossible for him at the Ambassador, *for such a thing as that all the prerequisites are lacking at the Ambassador*, Reger said. On the Bordone Room settee he was able to pick up the most complicated ideas and follow them through and eventually bring them together in an interesting result, but not at the Ambassador. But of course the Ambassador has a number of advantages which the Kunsthistorisches

Museum lacks, Reger said, not to mention the fact
that I am each time enchanted by the lavatory at the
Ambassador since that lavatory was recently rebuilt;
in Vienna, let me tell you, where all lavatories are in
fact more neglected than in any major city in Europe,
this is a rarity, to find a lavatory that does not turn
your stomach, where one need not, while using it,
hold one's eyes and nose firmly closed the whole time;
Viennese lavatories are altogether a scandal, even in
the lower Balkans you will not find a lavatory which
is quite so neglected, Reger said. Vienna has no
lavatory culture, he said, Vienna is one great lavatory
scandal, even at the most famous hotels in the city
there are scandalous lavatories, you find the most
ghastly pissoirs in Vienna, more ghastly than in any
other city, and if ever you have to pass water you get
the shock of your life. Vienna is quite superficially
famous for its opera, but in fact it is feared and detested
for its scandalous lavatories. The Viennese, and the
Austrians generally, have no lavatory culture, nowhere
in the world would you find such filthy and smelly
lavatories, Reger said. To have to go to the lavatory
in Vienna is usually a disaster, unless you are an acrobat
you get yourself filthy, and the stench there is such
that it clings to your clothes, often for weeks. The
Viennese are altogether dirty, Reger said, there are no
city-dwellers in Europe who are dirtier, just as it is a

well-known fact that the dirtiest flats in Europe are the Viennese flats; the Viennese flats are even dirtier, a lot dirtier, than the Viennese lavatories. The Viennese keep saying everything is so dirty in the Balkans, you hear this kind of talk everywhere, but Vienna is a hundred times dirtier than the Balkans, Reger said. When you accompany a Viennese to his flat your mind as a rule boggles at the dirt. Of course there are exceptions, but as a rule Viennese flats are the dirtiest flats in the world. I always wonder, what must those foreigners think when they have to go to the lavatory in Vienna, what must these people, who after all are used to clean lavatories, think when they have to use the dirtiest lavatories in the whole of Europe. The people only hurry to pass water and emerge from the pissoirs horrified at so much dirt. Everywhere also that horrible stench in every public lavatory, no matter whether you go to a lavatory at a railway station or whether you need to go in the Underground, you have to visit one of the dirtiest lavatories in Europe. In the Vienna cafés too, and especially there, the lavatories are so dirty you feel nauseated. On the one hand this megalomaniac cult of gigantic gateaux, and on the other these frightfully dirty lavatories, he said. With many of these lavatories you have the impression that they have not been cleaned for years. On the one hand the café proprietors protect their gateaux against even the slightest draught, which of course is of benefit to the gateaux, and on the other they attach not the slightest importance to the cleanliness of their lavatories. Just wait, Reger said, if you ever have to go to the lavatory at one of those, for the most part, rather famous cafés before you have started on your gateau, because when you return from the lavatory you will have lost all your appetite for eating even a mouthful of the gateau offered, or maybe even served, to you. And the Viennese restaurants, too, are dirty, I maintain that they are the dirtiest in the whole of Europe. Every other moment you are confronted with a totally bespattered tablecloth and when you draw a waiter's attention to the fact that the tablecloth is bespattered and that you do not intend to eat your meal off a tablecloth bespattered from one end to the other, that bespattered tablecloth is but reluctantly removed and replaced by a fresh one, by asking for a dirty tablecloth to be replaced then you merely attract furious and indeed dangerous glances. In most taverns you do not even get a tablecloth on your table and when you ask for at least the worst mess to be wiped off the dirty and very often even beer-wet table-top you invite an ill-mannered grumpy response, Reger said. The lavatory question and the tablecloth question are still unsolved in Vienna, Reger said. In every big city in the world, and I can say that I have visited nearly all of them and have come to know most of them more than just superficially, you get a clean tablecloth on your table as a matter of course before you start your meal. In Vienna a clean tablecloth or at least a clean table-top is anything but a matter of course. And it is the same with the lavatories, the Viennese lavatories are the most nauseating not only in Europe but in the whole world. What use to you is a superb meal if, even before you start eating, you lose your appetite in the lavatory, and what use to you is a superb meal if your stomach turns afterwards in the lavatory, he said. The Viennese, as indeed the Austrians, have no lavatory culture, an Austrian lavatory has always been a disaster, Reger said. Much as Vienna is famous for its mostly really excellent cuisine, at least as far as desserts are concerned, its renown with regard to its lavatories is inglorious. Until quite recently the Ambassador, too, had a lavatory which defied all description. But one day the management came to its senses and built a new one, an exceptionally well-planned one, in fact *a perfect one not only architecturally but down to the last hygienically sociological detail.* The Viennese are in fact the dirtiest people in Europe and it has been scientifically established that a Viennese uses a piece of soap only once a week, just as it has been scientifically established that he changes his underpants only once a week, just as he changes his shirt at most twice a week, and most Viennese change their bedlinen only once a month, Reger said. As for socks or stockings, a Viennese, on average, wears the same pair for twelve consecutive days, Reger said. In view of all this, manufacturers of soap and linen do worse business in Vienna, and of course throughout Austria, than anywhere else in Europe, Reger said. Instead the Viennese consume vast quantities of scent of the cheapest kind, Reger said, and they all reek from afar of violets or carnations or lilies of the valley or boxwood. And it is of course logical, from the external dirt of the Viennese, to draw conclusions about their inner dirt, Reger said, and the Viennese are in fact not much less dirty inside than outside and possibly, Reger said, I am saying possibly, that is not with complete certainty, he corrected himself, the Viennese are actually a lot dirtier inside than they are out. Everything suggests that they are a lot dirtier inside than out. But I do not feel like pursuing the subject, he then said, that would surely be a task for so-called sociologists, to do a study of the subject. Such a study would probably have to describe the dirtiest people in Europe, Reger suggested. You do not know how happy I am that there is this newly-built lavatory at the Ambassador; at the Kunsthistorisches Museum there is still the old one. As I am getting steadily older and not younger,

I have lately also had to visit the lavatory at the Kunst-historisches Museum with increasing frequency, Reger said, and this, under the conditions still prevailing here, is a nerve-racking unpleasant experience for me every day, because the lavatory at the Kunsthistorisches Museum is beneath contempt. Just as the lavatory at the Musikverein is beneath contempt. I even once permitted myself the joke of mentioning in one of my reviews for *The Times* that the lavatory at the Musikverein, that is in the supreme of all supreme Viennese temples of the Muses, defies description and that for this reason, for this scandalous lavatorial reason, Reger said, it always costs me some self-denial to go to the Musikverein, and that I very often ask myself at home whether or not I should go to the Musikverein, since at my age and with my kidneys I have to go to the lavatory at least twice during an evening at the Musikverein. But each time I have in fact gone to the Musikverein, because of Mozart and Beethoven, because of Berg and Schoenberg, because of Bartók and Webern, overcoming my lavatory phobia. How exceptional the music played at the Musikverein must have been, Reger said, for me to go there even though I have to visit the Musikverein lavatory at least twice during the evening. Art is merciless, I tell myself each time I enter the Musikverein lavatory, and so I enter it, Reger said. With eyes closed and my nose pinched as far as possible I pass water at the Musikverein lavatory, he said, this is quite a special art of its own which I have mastered with virtuosity for quite a while. Apart from the fact that the Viennese lavatories and the Viennese pissoirs are altogether the dirtiest in the world, with the exception of the so-called developing countries, nothing in them actually works as far as the sanitary equipment is concerned, there is either no water coming out of the taps, or else the water does not drain away, or else it neither runs in nor drains away, often for months on end no one cares whether the lavatories and pissoirs are functioning or not, Reger said. Probably the only way to improve this appalling state of Viennese lavatories would be for the city or the state, or whoever, to enact the strictest *lavatory and pissoir laws*, such rigorously strict laws that hoteliers and innkeepers and café proprietors would really have to maintain their lavatories and pissoirs. The hoteliers and innkeepers and café proprietors will not by themselves change this state of affairs, they will perpetuate this whole lavatory and pissoir mess into all eternity unless they are compelled by the city or the state to put their lavatories and pissoirs in order. Vienna is the city of music, I once wrote in *The Times*, but it is also the city of the most nauseating lavatories and pissoirs. London by now is aware of this fact, but Vienna of course is not, because the Viennese do not read *The Times*, they content themselves with all the most primitive and most ghastly papers printed anywhere in the world for the purpose of stultification, in other words they content themselves with the papers ideally appropriate to the perverse emotional and intellectual state of the Viennese. The Russian group had gone. The settee in the Bordone Room was empty. Reger, as I had seen, had got up after Irrsigler had whispered something in his ear and had walked out, his black hat, which he had kept on all the time, on his head. There were now two minutes to go to half-past eleven. The Russian group was standing in the so-called Veronese Room, the Ukrainian interpreter was now talking about Veronese, but what she was saying about Veronese she had already said about Bordone and Tintoretto, the same trivialities, the same twaddle, in the same cadences in the same disagreeable voice, she was speaking not only the usual feminine Russian which basically always gets on my nerves, but she was moreover speaking in that, to me almost unbearable, piercing falsetto so that all that while I actually suffered an acute pain in my auditory canal. A hearing such as mine is sensitive and it scarcely tolerates especially disagreeable female voices in that certain falsetto pitch. Why Irrsigler had not been seen for some time, when normally, in accordance with regulations, he had to look into the Bordone Room every so often, I could not understand, it certainly seemed very odd to me that he had left the Bordone Room along with Reger and had not returned for such a long time. But as I have an appointment with Reger in just this Bordone Room at half-past eleven and as Reger is the most punctual and most reliable person I know, Reger will return to the Bordone Room at half-past eleven precisely, I reflected, and no sooner had I so reflected than Reger actually returned to the Bordone Room, though not, before finally sitting down again on the Bordone Room settee, without looking around him in all directions; anticipating this I had, as soon as I became aware of him returning to the Bordone Room, withdrawn back to the Sebastiano Room; I therefore once more posted myself in the corner of the Sebastiano Room into which I had been pushed by the uncouth Russian group and from where I was able to observe Reger who had now returned to the Bordone Room, that mistrustful Reger, as I was thinking, who was still looking around in all directions in order to feel quite safe and who, among other things, had suffered all his life from a positively fatal persecution mania, which of course had always been useful to him without being really dangerous to him or to anyone else. Reger was now again seated on the Bordone Room settee, studying the *White-Bearded Man* by

Tintoretto. On the dot of half-past eleven he glanced at his pocket watch, which he had pulled from his jacket with lightning speed, and at the same moment I stepped out from the Sebastiano Room and into the Bordone Room and stopped in front of Reger. *Terrible, those Russian groups*, Reger said, *terrible, I hate those Russian groups*, he repeated. He commanded me formally to sit down on the Bordone Room settee, *come on, sit down next to me*, he said. *I am happy with every punctual person*, he said. *The majority of people are unpunctual, that is terrible. But you have always been punctual*, he said, *that is one of your great qualities*. If only you knew, he then said, what a bad night I had. I swallowed twice as many tablets as usual and still I slept badly. I constantly dreamt of my wife, I cannot get rid of those nightmares when I am dreaming of my wife. And I reflected about *you*, about how you have developed over these past few years. Strange how you have developed, he said. Basically you lead an unusual existence, a more or less totally independent one, allowing of course for the fact that there is no independent person on earth, let alone a totally independent one. If I did not have the Ambassador, he said, I would not survive the afternoons. Lately there have been so many Arabs going there it will soon be an *Arab hotel* when surely it has always been a *Jewish hotel, Jews and Hungarians, especially Hungarian*

Jews, that is what has made the hotel so agreeable to me over the years, he said, I do not even mind the Persian carpet dealers who pursue their carpet trade at the Ambassador. But don't you also think that gradually it is becoming dangerous to sit at the Ambassador, could not a bomb explode there at any moment, seeing that the hotel is constantly populated by Israeli Jews and by Egyptian Arabs? Good Lord, I wouldn't mind being blown up, so long as it was instantaneous. Spending the morning at the Kunsthistorisches Museum and the afternoon at the Ambassador, and having a good lunch at the Astoria or the Bristol, that is what I appreciate. Naturally I could not lead a life like this from *The Times* alone, he pretended, *The Times* more or less just sends me my pocket money to Austria. But the shares are not doing well, the stock market is a disaster. And life in Austria is getting more expensive every day. On the other hand I have calculated that, provided no so-called *Third World War* breaks out, I can without any problem easily live for another two decades on what I have. That is reassuring, even though it all shrinks from day to day. You are the typical private scholar, Atzbacher, he said to me, indeed you are the quintessence of the private scholar, you are altogether the quintessence of the private *person*, utterly out of step with our time, Reger said. That is what I was thinking again today as I climbed those frightful stairs up to the Bordone Room, that you are *the genuine and typical private person*, probably the only one I know and I know a lot of people who are all private persons but *you are the typical, the genuine one.* The way you can bear working for decades on a single book without publishing the least part of it, I could not do that. I must enjoy the publication of my work at least once a month, he said, this habit is an indispensable need and that is why I am happy with *The Times* for regularly meeting me in this habit and moreover paying me for it. After all, he said, I enjoy writing, those brief works of art which are never longer than two pages, which always means three and a half columns in *The Times*, he said. Have you never considered publishing at least a minor section of your work? he asked; some fragment, it all sounds so excellent, your hints about your work, on the other hand it is also a *supreme joy not to publish, nothing at all*, he said. But some time surely you will want to know what effect your work produces, he said, and you will publish at least part of your work. On the one hand it is magnificent to hold back, as it were, with the work of a lifetime and not to publish it, and on the other it is just as magnificent to publish. I am a congenital publishing person, while you are a congenital non-publishing person. Probably your work and yourself, and hence your work in relation to yourself and you in relation to your work, are condemned to non-publication, because surely you are suffering all the time by working on your subject without publishing your work, that is the truth, I think, you just will not admit it, not even to yourself, that you are suffering from this, as I call it, non-publication compulsion. Myself, I would suffer from not publishing my writing. But of course your writing cannot be compared to my writing. Admittedly I do not know any writer, or at least any writing person, who could, for any length of time, bear *not* to publish what he has written, who would not be curious to know the public's reaction to what he has written, I am always consumed with curiosity, Reger said, even though I always say I am not consumed with curiosity and it does not interest me. I do not care about the opinion of the public, I am in fact consumed by curiosity and I am lying when I say I am not consumed with curiosity when in fact I am consumed with curiosity, I admit it, I am always consumed with curiosity, ceaselessly, he said. I want to know what people are saying about what I have written, he said, I want to know all the time about everyone, even though I keep saying I am not interested in what people are saying, and that it does not interest me, that it leaves me cold, yet I am consumed with curiosity all the time and wait for it with the tensest expectation, he said. I am lying when I say I am not interested in public opinion, I am not interested in my readers, I am lying when I say I do not wish to know what people think about what I have written or that I do not read what is being written about it. I am lying when I say this, lying most shamelessly, he said, because I am ceaselessly consumed with curiosity to know what people are saying about what I have written, I want to know it always and at all times, and I am affected by it, by whatever people are saying about what I have written, that is the truth. Of course I only hear what *The Times* people say about it and what they say is not always only flattering, Reger said, but as far as you are concerned, as a philosophical writer, as it were, surely you should be just as much consumed with curiosity to know what people are saying about your philosophical writings, what they think about them, I just do not understand you not publishing your writings at least in excerpts, if only to discover for once what the public, or, as it were, the competent public, thinks about them, even though at the same time I have to admit that there is no such thing as a competent public, there is no such thing as competence, there never was and there never will be; but does it not depress you to write and write and to think and think and to write down what you think and write it down again, and the whole thing without an echo?

he said. You are bound to miss a lot through your obstinate non-publishing, he said, maybe even something crucial. You have been working at your opus for decades now and you say you are writing this work *solely for yourself, that is appalling*, no one writes a work for himself, if someone says he is writing only for himself then that is a lie, but you know just as well as I do that there are no greater or worse liars than those who write, the world, as long as it exists, has not known any greater liars than those who write, none more vain and none more false, Reger said. If you knew what a frightful night I have had again, time and again I had to get up with frightful cramp from my toes upwards through my calves all the way to my thorax, from those diuretic tablets I have to take because of my heart. I find myself in a vicious circle, he said. Every night is a horror to me, whenever I think now I can go to sleep I get those cramps and have to get up and pace up and down my room. All night I have more or less paced up and down and when I have been able to go to sleep I was immediately wakened by those nightmares I mentioned to you. In these nightmares I dream of my wife, it is terrible. I have had these nightmares ever since her death, ceaselessly, I have them every night. Believe me, I always very nearly think that it might have been better if, with my wife's death, I had put an end to things myself. I cannot forgive myself for that cowardice. This continuous and by now pathological self-pity is unbearable to me, but I cannot shake myself out of it, he said. If at least there were a decent concert at the Musikverein, he said, but the winter programme is terrible, they are only doing stale and hackneyed things, forever those Mozart concertos and Brahms concertos and Beethoven concertos which by now get on my nerves, all those Mozart and Brahms and Beethoven cycles have become insufferable. And at the Opera dilettantism is rampant. If the Opera were at least interesting, but at the moment it is totally uninteresting, bad repertoire, bad singers and a miserable orchestra to boot. Think of the Philharmonic a mere two or three years ago, he said, and what are they today, *a run-of-the-mill-orchestra*. Just imagine, last week I heard the *Winterreise* sung by a Leipzig bass, I won't mention his name, it would not actually mean anything to you, after all you are not interested in *theoretical music* at all, you are lucky, he said, that bass was a disaster. Always inevitably *The Crow*, he said, it is insufferable. Such a recital is not worth dressing for, I regretted my clean shirt. *I do not write in The Times about such rubbish*, he said. *Mahler, Mahler, Mahler*, he said, *that too is enervating.* But the Mahler vogue has passed its peak, thank God, he said, Mahler really is the most overrated composer of the century. Mahler was an excellent conductor, but he is a mediocre composer, like all good conductors, like, for example, Hindemith, and like Klemperer. The Mahler vogue was something awful for me all these years, the whole world was in a positive Mahler delirium, it was unbearable. And did you know that my wife's grave, where I too will be buried, is right next to Mahler's grave? Oh well, at the cemetery it really is a matter of indifference whom one is lying next to, even to lie next to Mahler does not worry me. *Das Lied von der Erde* with Kathleen Ferrier, perhaps, Reger said, anything else by Mahler I reject, it is not worth anything, it does not stand up to closer examination. By comparison Webern is truly a genius, not to mention Schoenberg and Berg. No, Mahler was an aberration. Mahler is the typical *art nouveau* fashion composer, needless to say a lot worse than Bruckner, who has quite a few kitschy similarities with Mahler. At this time of year Vienna has nothing to offer to a person with intellectual interests, and unfortunately very little to one with musical interests, he said. But of course the foreigners who come to the city are easily satisfied, they go to the Opera regardless of what is on, even if it is the worst rubbish, and they attend the most ghastly concerts and clap their hands sore and, as you can see, they even stream into the Natural Science Museum and into the Kunsthistorisches

Museum. Civilized humanity's hunger for culture is enormous, the perversity reflected by this state of affairs is worldwide. Vienna is a cultural concept, Reger said, even though there has virtually been no culture in Vienna for a long time, and one day there will really be no culture of any kind left in Vienna, but it will nevertheless be a cultural concept even then. Vienna will always be a cultural concept, it will the more stubbornly be a cultural concept the less culture there is in it. And soon there will really be no culture left in this city, he said. These progressively more stupid governments which we have here in Austria will gradually see to it that soon there is no culture of any kind left in Austria, only philistinism, Reger said. The atmosphere here in Austria is getting ever more anti-cultural and everything points to the fact that before very long Austria will be a totally culture-less country. But I shall not live to see that depressing end of the trend, *you may*, Reger said, you may live to see it, but I won't, I am too old now to live to see the final decline and actual culture-lessness in Austria. The light of culture will be extinguished in Austria, believe me, the dull-wittedness which has been at the helm in this country for so long will before long extinguish the light of culture. Then it will be dark in Austria, Reger said. But you can say what you like in this respect, no one will listen to you, you will be regarded as a fool.

What use is there in my writing in *The Times* what I think of Austria and what, sooner or later but within the foreseeable future, is happening to Austria? No use, Reger said, not the least. A pity I won't live to see it, I mean the Austrians fumbling about in the dark because their light of culture has gone out. A pity I won't be able to participate, he said. You may wonder why I asked you to come here again today. There is a reason. But I won't tell you the reason until later. I do not know *how* to tell you the reason. I do not know. I think about it all the time and I do not know. I have been here for hours, thinking about it and I do not know. Irrsigler is my witness, Reger said, I have been sitting here on the settee for hours, wondering *how* to tell you *why* I have asked you to come to the Kunsthistorisches Museum *again today. Later, later*, Reger said, *give me time.* We commit a crime and are unable to report it quite simply without ado, Reger said. Give me time to calm down, he said, I have already told Irrsigler but I cannot tell you yet, he said, it really is disgraceful. By the way, what I said to you yesterday about the so-called *Tempest Sonata* is certainly interesting and I am also certain that what I said to you about that so-called *Tempest Sonata* is correct, but it is probably more interesting to me than it is to you. This is what always happens when we talk about a subject because the subject fascinates us, but it fascinates us more than the person on whom, when all is said and done, we force it with all the frantic ruthlessness we are capable of. I forced these views on the so-called *Tempest Sonata* upon you yesterday, that is a fact. In connection with my lecture on the Art of the Fugue, he said, I found it necessary also to examine the *Tempest Sonata* and yesterday I was feeling in a positively ideal state for it and I made *you the victim of my musicological passion*, as indeed I very frequently make you the victim of my musicological passion because I have no other person equally suitable for it. I very often think, *you have come at just the right moment, what would I do without you*, he said. Yesterday I troubled you with the *Tempest Sonata*, who knows what piece of music I may trouble you with the day after tomorrow, he said, there are so many musicological subjects in my head which I am most anxious to elucidate; but I need a listener, a victim as it were, for my compulsive musicological talking, he said, because my continuous talk about musicological topics is certainly *a kind of musicological compulsive talk*. Everybody has his own, his *very* own, compulsive talk, mine is musicological. I have had this musicological compulsive talk all my musicological life, because my life undoubtedly is nothing but musicological, just as yours is philosophical, that much is obvious. Of course I could say today that everything I said to you about the *Tempest Sonata yesterday* is nonsense *today*, since everything that is said is nonsense, *but we do utter that nonsense convincingly*, Reger said. Anything that is said sooner or later turns out to be nonsense, but if we utter it convincingly, with the most incredible vehemence we can muster, then it is no crime, he said. Anything we think we also wish to utter, Reger said, and basically we do not rest until we have uttered it, because if we keep silent about it we choke on it. Mankind would have choked long ago if it had kept silent about all the nonsense it thought throughout its history, any individual who keeps silent too long chokes, and mankind too cannot remain silent too long because it would otherwise choke, even though what the individual thinks or what mankind thinks and what every individual has ever thought and what mankind has ever thought is nothing but nonsense. Sometimes we are masters of speech and sometimes we are masters of silence and we perfect our mastery to the utmost, he said, our lives are interesting in exactly the measure to which we have succeeded in developing our mastery of speech and our mastery of silence. *The Tempest Sonata is not really a great work*, Reger said, on close consideration it is merely one of the many so-called secondary works, basically a piece of kitsch. The quality of the piece consists more in the fact that it lends itself to discussion than in itself.

Beethoven was absolutely the monotonous cramped artist as a man of violence, not necessarily what I esteem most highly. To analyse the *Tempest Sonata* has always amused me, it is the most doom-laden piece by Beethoven, through the *Tempest Sonata* Beethoven can be clearly presented, his nature, his genius, his kitsch all emerge clearly, and his limitations are shown up. But I only spoke about the *Tempest Sonata* because yesterday I wanted to elucidate the Art of the Fugue to you more extensively and more intensively, and for that it was necessary to draw on the *Tempest Sonata*, Reger said. Incidentally, I hate such labels as *Tempest Sonata* or *Eroica* or *Unfinished* or *Surprise*, such labels are distasteful to me. Like saying *The Magus of the North*, that is utterly distasteful to me, Reger said. Just because you have really no *theoretical* interest whatever in music you are the ideal victim for my discussions on music, Reger said. You *listen attentively and do not contradict*, he said, you leave me to talk, that is what I need, never mind what it is worth, it smoothes my path through this dreadful musical existence, believe me, one that in fact very rarely provides happiness. What I think is enervating, destructive, he said, on the other hand it has been enervating me for so long and destroying me for so long that I need no longer fear it. I thought you would be punctual and you are punctual, he said, I do not expect you to be anything but punctual, and punctuality, as you know, is what I appreciate above all else, wherever there are human beings there must be punctuality and, making common cause with punctuality, reliability, he said. Half-past eleven and you stepped into the room, he said, I looked at my watch and it was half-past eleven and just then you stood before me. I have *no other person more useful than you*, he said. Probably survival has been possible for me only thanks to you. I should not have said this, Reger said, to say this is a piece of impertinence, he said, of unparalleled impertinence, but I have said it, you are the person who enables me to go on existing, I really have no one else. And did you know that my wife was very fond of you? She never told you but she told me, more than once. You have a clear head, Reger said, that is the most precious thing in the world. You are a loner and you have preserved your lonerdom, go on preserving it as long as you live, Reger said. I slipped into art to get away from life, that is how I might put it. I sneaked off into art, he said. I waited for the most favourable moment and I used that most favourable moment and sneaked off, out of the world into art, into music, he said. As others might sneak off into painting or sculpture or into acting. These people who, like myself, basically *really hate the world*, sneak off from one moment to the next from the world they hate, and into art which is totally apart from that hated world. I sneaked off into music, he said, all very surreptitiously. Because I had the opportunity, whereas most people do not have that opportunity. You sneaked off into philosophy and authorship, Reger said, but you are neither a philosopher nor an author, that is what is simultaneously so interesting and so unfortunate *about you and in you*, because you are not really a philosopher and not really an author either, because for a philosopher you lack everything that is characteristic of a philosopher, and for an author similarly everything, even though you are exactly what I call the philosophical writer, your philosophy is no real philosophy and your writing is no real writing, he repeated. And a writer who does not publish anything is, basically, not really a writer. You probably suffer from *publication phobia*, Reger said, *a publishing trauma has caused you not to want to publish*. At the Ambassador yesterday you were wearing such a well-cut sheepskin coat which surely came from Poland, he suddenly said, and I said, yes, you are right, I was wearing a Polish sheepskin coat, as you know I have been to Poland a number of times, Poland is one of my two favourite countries, I love Poland and I love Portugal, I said, but Poland probably more than Portugal, and on my last visit to Cracow, but it must be eight or nine years since I was in Cracow, I bought that sheepskin coat, I specially travelled to the Russian frontier in order to buy it, because only on the Polish–Russian frontier do these sheepskin coats have that cut. Yes, Reger said, it is indeed a pleasure to see a well-dressed person now and again, a well-dressed good-looking person, especially when the weather is so gloomy and one's head more or less in gloom and one's mood altogether at rock-bottom. Occasionally you can now see well-dressed and good-looking people even in this down-at-heel Vienna, for many years you saw in Vienna nothing but people in tasteless clothes, those depressing mass-produced goods. Now a touch of colour seems to have come into clothes again, he said, but there are *so few well-built people*, you walk for hours through this down-at-heel Vienna and see *nothing but depressing faces and tasteless clothes*, as if *only crippled people* were passing you all the time. The lack of taste and the monotony of the Viennese depressed me for decades. I used to think that only in Germany were they so monotonous and lacking in taste, but the Viennese are just as monotonous and lacking in taste. Only quite recently has the picture changed, people are generally looking better, they are again wearing individual clothes, he said, when you are wearing that sheepskin coat you cut an impressive figure, Reger said. One sees so few well-dressed *and* intelligent people, he said. For many years I only walked through this down-at-heel Vienna with my head sunk between my shoulders because I could not bear to see so much mass ugliness in the streets, those masses of tasteless people walking towards one were simply unbearable. Those hundreds of thousands of the industrially clothed who stifled me during my very first steps in the streets, he said. And not only in the so-called proletarian districts, also in the so-called Inner City, the city centre, those grey industrially clothed human masses stifled me, especially in the Inner City, he said. Young people nowadays, though still tasteless, go out into the streets in very cheerful colours, as if all these people had only just, forty years after its conclusion, overcome the war, the war trauma, Reger said, which had made people appear so grey and insignificant for nearly forty years. But of course you see a well-dressed person only, as the phrase goes, once in a blue moon in this down-at-heel Vienna. That of course makes you feel good, he said, and then: *Only Gould ever played the Tempest Sonata really well and made it tolerable, no one else.* Anyone else made it intolerable to me. *It is, of course, very ponderous, the Tempest Sonata,* Reger said, like a lot of Beethoven's work. But even Mozart did not escape kitsch, especially in the operas there is so much kitsch, the coy and the frisky often turn somersaults in the most unbearable way in those superficial operas. A turtle-dove here, a turtle-dove there, a raised forefinger here, a raised forefinger there, Reger said, that *too* is Mozart. Mozart's music is also full of petticoat and frilly undies kitsch, he said. And the state composer Beethoven, as the *Tempest Sonata* above all demonstrates, is *positively ridiculously serious*. But where would it get us if we subjected everything to this deadly kind of examination, Reger said. Fussiness and kitsch, after all, are the two principal characteristics of so-called civilized man, highly stylized as he has become into a single human grotesque over hundreds and thousands of years, he said. Anything human is kitschy, he said, there can be no doubt about that. And so is high art and the highest art. Returning from London to Vienna, when in fact he had felt more at home in London than in Vienna, had been a real shock to him. But I could not have remained in London under any circumstances, if only because of my unstable health, which has always been close to flipping over into a dangerous disease, a fatal disease, Reger said. In London I had lived, in Vienna I have never truly lived, in London my head felt well, in Vienna my head never really felt well, in London I had my best ideas, he said. My time in London was my best time, he said. In London I always had all the opportunities I never had in Vienna, he said. After the death of my parents it was a matter of course for me to return to Vienna, to this grey war-depressed, spiritless city in which initially I existed for several years but only in a state of shock. But at the moment when I did no longer know which way to turn I met my wife, he said. My wife saved me; I had always been afraid of the female sex and *in fact* in a manner of speaking *hated women body and soul* and yet, he said, his wife had saved him. And do you know where I met my wife? he asked; have I ever told you? he asked, and I thought that he had often told me but did not say so and he said, *I met my wife at the Kunsthistorisches Museum. And do you know where in the Kunsthistorisches Museum?* he asked, and I thought of course I know where in the Kunsthistorisches Museum and he said, *here in the Bordone Room, on this settee,* he said this as if he really did not know that he had told me a hundred times that he had met his wife on the Bordone Room settee and I pretended, as he told me again, that I had *never before* heard it. *It was a gloomy day,* he said, *I was in despair, I was studying Schopenhauer very thoroughly at the time, having lost all interest in Descartes, as indeed, then, in French thought generally, and I was sitting here on this settee, meditating, over a particular sentence of Schopenhauer's, I cannot now tell you which sentence,* he said. Suddenly some headstrong woman sat down on the settee next to me and remained there. I had made a signal to Irrsigler, but Irrsigler at first did not understand what my signal was intended to mean and subsequently proved unable to induce the woman sitting next to me to get up and leave, the woman was sitting there, staring at the *White-Bearded Man*, Reger said, and I believe she stared at the *White-Bearded Man* for an hour. Do you really like Tintoretto's *White-Bearded Man* that much? I asked the woman sitting next to me, Reger said, *and at first I received no answer to my question.* Only after a long while did the woman utter a *No* which truly fascinated me, *a No such as I had never heard before this No,* Reger said. So you do not like Tintoretto's *White-Bearded Man* at all? I asked the woman. No, I do not like him, the woman replied. A conversation, as I have said, then developed about art, in particular painting, about the old masters, Reger said, and suddenly I had no wish to cut the conversation short for a long time yet, throughout that conversation I was interested not in its content but *in the way it was conducted.* In the end, after prolonged reflection one way and another, I proposed to the woman that I take her to lunch at the *Astoria* and she accepted, and not very much later we were married. Then it turned out that she was also very wealthy, being the owner of several shops in the Inner City, also of blocks of flats on the Singerstrasse and on the Spiegelgasse, and indeed of one on the Kohlmarkt, he said. In addition to everything else. *Suddenly I had a wife who was an intelligent, wealthy cosmopolitan,* Reger said, who saved me with her intelligence and with her wealth, because my wife did save me, I was, as the saying goes, *down and out* when I met my wife, he said. As you see, I owe a lot to the Kunsthistorisches Museum, he said. Maybe it is actually gratitude that makes me go to the Kunsthistorisches Museum every other day, he said with a laugh, but of course it is not that. Do you know that in my wife's so-called Himmelstrasse house in Grinzing there was a safe large enough for several people to walk into without difficulty? he said. In this safe she kept the most valuable Stradivarius, Guarneri and Maggini, he said. In addition to everything else. Like me, my wife had spent the war in London and it is most astonishing that I did not make her acquaintance in London, because my wife was then, that is at the same time, moving in the same London circles as I was. For years we had passed one another in London, Reger said. Incidentally, before we were married, my wife donated several paintings to the Kunsthistorisches Museum, Reger said, including a very valuable and not at all unsuccessful Furini, which by the way you will find right next to the Cigoli and the Empoli, which incidentally I do not care for at all. After our marriage my wife donated no more pictures, he said, I made her see that there was no point in making presents, making presents is altogether distasteful, he said. Just imagine, before we were married my wife made a present of a Biedermeier town panorama of Vienna, I think by Gauermann, to one of her nieces. A year later, when, more by accident than out of interest, merely, as it were, to kill time between two meals, she walked round the *Museum der Stadt Wien*, the Museum of the City of Vienna, she discovered in that Museum of the City of Vienna, which, in my opinion, is absolutely worthless, the Gauermann she had given to her niece. You can imagine the shock this was to her. She went straight to the management of the museum and learned that her niece had *sold* the picture, within a few weeks if not a few days of receiving it as a present from her aunt, my future wife, to the *Museum of the City of Vienna* for two hundred thousand schillings. Giving presents is one of the worst kinds of foolishness, Reger said. I very soon made my wife see that this is so and she never gave any presents of any kind afterwards. We tear an object which is dear to us, an object to which, as the phrase goes, our heart is attached, we tear a work of art out of our life, and the recipient goes along and sells it for a shameless, for a horrendous sum, Reger said. Giving presents is a terrible habit, motivated of course by a guilty conscience and very often also by a widespread fear of loneliness, Reger said, a wicked malpractice, and the present, the gift received, is not appreciated because it should have been more, and more still, and it ultimately only creates hatred, he said. I have never in my life given presents, he said, but I have also always declined to accept presents, indeed I have all my life been afraid of *being given* presents. And do you know that Irrsigler too had a part in my marriage? Irrsigler, as it subsequently turned out, had suggested to my wife, who was suddenly leaning, utterly exhausted, against the wall in the Sebastiano Room, that she should sit down for a while in the Bordone Room on the Bordone Room settee, Irrsigler had led her from the Sebastiano Room into the Bordone Room, and on his advice she had sat down on the Bordone Room settee, Reger said. If Irrsigler had not led her into the Bordone Room I probably would have never met her, Reger said. You know that I do not believe in chance, he said. Seen in this light, Irrsigler was our match-maker, Reger said. For a long time my wife and I never realized that basically Irrsigler had been our match-maker, until one day, during a reconstruction of our relationship, we discovered it. Irrsigler once said that he had *observed* my future wife for quite a while that time in the Sebastiano Room, he had not quite realized the reason for her, to him at first, *odd behaviour*, it had even occurred to him that she might be about to photograph one of the paintings hanging in the Sebastiano Room, which is strictly forbidden, that in her exceptionally large handbag, a handbag *forbidden in the museum*, she might have a camera, that is what he thought at first, only later did he realize that she was simply utterly exhausted. People always make the mistake in museums of embarking on too much, of wishing to see *everything*, so they walk and walk and look and look and then suddenly, because they have devoured a surfeit of art, they collapse. That is what happened to my future wife when Irrsigler took her by the arm and led her to the Bordone Room, as we subsequently established, in the most courteous manner, Reger said. The layman in matters of art goes to a museum and makes it nauseous for himself through excess, Reger said. But of course no advice is possible where visiting a museum is concerned. The expert goes to a museum in order to view at most *one* picture, Reger said, *one* statue, *one* object, Reger said, he goes to the museum to look at, to study, *one* Veronese, *one* Velazquez. But these art experts are all utterly distasteful to me, Reger said, they make a bee-line for a single work of art and examine it in their shameless unscrupulous way and walk out of the museum again, I hate those people, Reger said. On the other hand my stomach also turns when I see the layman in the museum, the way he devours everything uncritically, maybe the whole of occidental painting in one morning, as we can witness here day after day.

My wife had what is known as a *crise de conscience* the day I made her acquaintance, chasing through the Inner City for several hours she did not know whether to buy a coat from the firm of Braun or a suit from the firm of Knize. Thus torn between the firm of Braun and the firm of Knize she eventually decided to buy neither a coat from the firm of Braun nor a suit from the firm of Knize but instead to go to the Kunsthistorisches Museum, where until that day she had been only once, in her early childhood, holding on to her father, who was very keen on art. Irrsigler of course is aware of his role of matchmaker, Reger said. If Irrsigler had brought some other woman into the Bordone Room, I often reflect, Reger said, an entirely different woman, Reger repeated, *an Englishwoman or a Frenchwoman, it does not bear thinking about,* he said. We sit on this settee, utterly desolate, Reger said, more or less depression personified, hopelessness, Reger suggested, and a woman is placed next to us and we marry her and are saved. Millions of married couples have met on a seat, Reger said, indeed this is one of the most fatuous situations imaginable, and yet it is to this fatuous ludicrous situation that I owe my existence, because without meeting my wife I could not have continued to exist, as I now realize more clearly than ever before. For years I had sat on this settee in more or less the deepest despair and suddenly I was saved. I therefore owe to Irrsigler virtually everything that I am, for without Irrsigler I would have long ceased to be here, Reger said at the moment when Irrsigler looked into the Bordone Room from the Sebastiano Room. Towards twelve o'clock the Kunsthistorisches Museum is usually fairly empty, and on this day too there were not many people to be seen about any more and in the so-called Italian Department there was no one left except us. Irrsigler took one step from the Sebastiano Room into the Bordone Room as if to give Reger a chance to voice a request, but Reger had no request and so Irrsigler immediately withdrew again into the Sebastiano Room, he actually backed out of the Bordone Room into the Sebastiano Room. Irrsigler was closer to him than any close relative had ever been, Reger remarked, *there is more linking me to that man than ever linked me to one of my relatives*, he said. We have always managed to keep our relationship in an ideal equilibrium, Reger said, *in this ideal equilibrium for decades.* Irrsigler always feels protected by me, even though he has no clear idea in what respect he is being protected by me, just as I in turn always feel protected by Irrsigler, *naturally also without any idea of the actual connection*, Reger said. I am linked to Irrsigler in the most ideal way, Reger said, *it is a positively ideal remote relationship*, he remarked. Of course Irrsigler knows nothing about me, Reger said next, and it would be utter nonsense to tell him more about myself, *it is just because he knows nothing about me that our relationship is so ideal, just because I myself know as good as nothing about him*, Reger said, because all I know about Irrsigler is outward banalities, just as in turn he only knows me from outside in the most banal manner. We should not penetrate into a person with whom we have an ideal relationship more than we have already penetrated, otherwise we destroy that ideal relationship, Reger said. Here Irrsigler calls the tune, Reger said, and I am entirely in his hands, if Irrsigler today said to me, Herr Reger, from today you will no longer sit on this settee there is nothing I can do about it, Reger said, because after all it is madness to come to the Kunsthistorisches Museum for thirty years and to occupy the Bordone Room settee. I do not believe that Irrsigler has ever informed his superiors of the fact that I have been coming to the Kunsthistorisches Museum for thirty years and have been sitting on the Bordone Room settee every other day, I am sure he has not, from what I know of him he realizes that he *must* not do so, that the administration *must* not know about it. People are always very ready to send a person like me to the lunatic asylum, that is to Steinhof, when they learn that a person has been going to the Kunsthistorisches Museum for thirty years in order to sit on the Bordone Room settee every other day. That would be a real gift to the psychiatrists, Reger said. To get into a lunatic asylum a person has no need to sit on the Bordone Room settee every other day for thirty years, in front of Tintoretto's *White-Bearded Man*, it would be quite enough for a person to *have this habit for a mere two or three weeks, yet I have had this habit for over thirty years*, Reger said. *And I never gave up the habit when I got married, on the contrary, with my wife I even intensified this habit of going to the Kunsthistorisches Museum every other day and sitting on the Bordone Room settee.* I would be a *welcome gift, a real gold mine*, as the saying goes, for the psychiatrists, but the psychiatrists will not be given an opportunity to have me as a welcome gift and a gold mine, Reger said. After all, there are thousands of people in psychiatric hospitals who, so to speak, have committed some crazy act which is not nearly as crazy as mine, Reger said. There are people detained in psychiatric hospitals who just once *failed* to raise their hand when they should have raised it, Reger said, who just once said White instead of Black, Reger said, just try to imagine that. But I am not really crazy, he said, I am just a person of extraordinary habits, a person with one extraordinary habit, to wit the extraordinary habit of going to the Kunsthistorisches Museum every other day for the past thirty years and of sitting on the Bordone Room settee. Whereas to my wife it was *at first a frightful habit*, over the last years it *eventually* became *an agreeable habit* to her, whenever I asked her about it, she always said it was an agreeable habit for her to go with me to the Kunsthistorisches Museum, to our *White-Bearded Man* by Tintoretto and to sit on the Bordone Room settee, Reger said. I do in fact believe that the Kunsthistorisches Museum is the only refuge left to me, Reger said, I *have to go to the old masters to be able to continue to exist, precisely to these so-called old masters*, who have long, that is for decades, been abhorrent to me, because basically nothing is more abhorrent to me than these so-called old masters here at the Kunsthistorisches Museum and old masters generally, all old masters, no matter what their names are, no matter what they have painted, Reger said, and yet it is they who keep me alive. I walk through the city and I think that I cannot bear living in this city any longer and that I not only cannot bear the city any longer but that I cannot bear the whole world and in consequence the whole of mankind any longer, because the world and all mankind have meanwhile become so ghastly that soon they will no longer be bearable, at least not for a person such as me. For a man of intellect just as for a man of sensitivity like me the world and mankind will soon no longer be bearable, believe me, Atzbacher. I no longer find in this world and among these people anything that I appreciate, he said, everything in this world is dull-witted and everything in this mankind is just as dull-witted. This world and our mankind have now reached a degree of dull-wittedness which a person like myself can no longer afford, he said, such a person can no longer live in such a world, such a person can no longer coexist with such a mankind, Reger said. Everything in this world and in our mankind has been dulled down to the lowest level, Reger said, everything in this world has reached such a degree of public danger and base brutality that I am finding it well-nigh impossible to go on living even for a single day at a time in this world and in our mankind. Such a degree of low dull-wittedness had not been thought possible even by the most clear-sighted thinkers in history, Reger said, not by Schopenhauer, not by Nietzsche, not to mention Montaigne, Reger said, and as for our outstanding world poets, our poets of mankind, what they have predicted for the world and for mankind in terms of horror and decline is nothing compared to the actual state at present. Even Dostoyevsky, one of our greatest clairvoyants, described the future merely as a ludicrous idyll, just as Diderot only described a ludicrous idyll of the future. Dostoyevsky's terrible hell is so harmless compared with the one in which we find ourselves today that we only feel a cold shiver running down our spines when we think of it, and the same applies to the hell predicted and pre-described by Diderot. The one, from his Russian and West-Eastern point of view, no more foresaw or predicted or pre-described this absolute hell than his Western counter-thinker and counter-writer Diderot, Reger said. The world and mankind have arrived at a state of hell, such as the world and mankind have never before arrived at throughout history, that is the truth, Reger said. What these great thinkers and these great writers have pre-described is a positive idyll, Reger said, all of them, while believing that they were describing hell, merely described an idyll, a positively idyllic idyll compared to the hell in which we now exist, Reger said. Everything today is full of baseness and full of malice, lies and betrayal, Reger said, mankind has never been as shameless and perfidious as today. We may look at whatever we please, we may go wherever we please, we only look at malice and infamy and at betrayal and lies and hypocrisy and forever only at nothing but absolute baseness, no matter where we look, no matter where we go we are confronted with malice and with lies and with hypocrisy. What else do we see but lies and malice, hypocrisy and betrayal, the meanest baseness, whenever we walk out into the street, *when we dare to walk out into the street*, Reger said. We go out into the street and we walk into baseness, he said, into baseness and shamelessness, into hypocrisy and malice. We say that there is no country more mendacious and none more hypocritical and none more malicious than this country, yet when we leave this country, or even look beyond it, we see that outside our country too there reigns nothing but malice and hypocrisy and lies and baseness. We have the most distasteful government imaginable, the most hypocritical, the most malicious, the meanest and, at the same time, the stupidest, that is what we say and of course what we believe is true, and we say so at every other moment, Reger said, but when we look out from this mean, hypocritical and malicious and mendacious and stupid country we find that other countries are just as mendacious and hypocritical and altogether just as mean, said Reger. But those other countries are not really our concern, Reger said, *we are concerned with our country alone* and that is why we are *so* stunned each day that we have long come to exist *actually stunned* in a country whose government is mean and dull-witted and hypocritical and mendacious and utterly stupid to boot. Every day, if we think, we are aware of nothing so much as that we are governed by a hypocritical and mendacious and mean government, which moreover is the stupidest government imaginable, Reger said, and we think that we can do nothing about it, that really is the most terrible thing, that we can do nothing about it, that we simply have to watch impotently as this government is getting ever more mendacious and more hypocritical and meaner and baser every day, that we have to watch in a more or less permanent state of dismay as this government is getting progressively worse and progressively more unbearable. But not only the government is mendacious and hypocritical and mean and base, parliament is so too, Reger said, and sometimes it seems to me that parliament is yet a lot more hypocritical and mendacious than the government, and think how mendacious and how mean the judiciary is in this country and the press in this country and eventually culture in this country and eventually everything in this country; nothing but mendaciousness and hypocrisy and meanness and baseness have reigned in this country for decades, Reger said. This country has in fact now reached an absolute low, Reger said, and before long it will have given up its meaning and purpose and its ghost. And everywhere that nauseating twaddle of democracy! You walk out into the street, he remarked, and you constantly have to shut your eyes and ears and even hold your nose pinched in order to be able to survive in this country which has eventually become a positively dangerous state, Reger said. Any day you can scarcely believe your eyes and you can scarcely believe your ears, he said, any day you experience the decline of this ruined country and of this corrupt state and of this stultified people with an ever greater shock. And the people in this country and in this state are doing nothing about it, Reger said, that is what torments someone like me every day. Of course the people see or feel how this state is debasing itself every day and becoming meaner every day, but they are not doing anything about it. The politicians are the murderers, indeed the mass murderers of every country and of every state, Reger said, the politicians have been murdering the countries and the states for centuries and there is no one to stop them. And we Austrians have the most cunning and at the same time most brainless politicians as murderers of our country and state, Reger said. Politicians as state murderers are at the head of our state, politicians as state murderers sit in our parliament, he said, that is the truth. Every chancellor and every minister is a state murderer and hence also a national murderer, Reger said, and when one of them departs another arrives, Reger said, when one murderer departs as chancellor, another chancellor arrives as a murderer, when one minister departs as a state murderer another arrives at once. The people are always a people murdered by politicians, Reger said, but the people do not see it, admittedly they feel that this is how things are but they do not see any of it, that is the tragedy, Reger said. No sooner do we rejoice that one state murderer has gone as chancellor than another arrives, Reger said, it is horrible. The politicians are state murderers and national murderers, and they murder while they are in power, unabashed, and the state judiciary supports their vile and infamous murdering, their vile and infamous abuse. But of course every people and every society deserves the state they have, and they therefore deserve also its murderers as politicians, Reger said. Those mean and dull-witted state abusers and mean and perfidious abusers of democracy, he exclaimed. The politicians dominate the Austrian scene absolutely, Reger then said, the state murderers dominate the Austrian scene absolutely. Political conditions in this country are at present so depressing that one might expect them to give one nothing but sleepless nights, but then all other Austrian conditions are nowadays just as depressing. If by any chance you came into contact with the judiciary you will find that it is nothing but a corrupt and vile and mean judiciary, not to mention the fact that so-called *miscarriages of justice* have been piling up on an alarming scale over the past few years, hardly a week passes without some long-closed proceedings being reopened because of *serious procedural errors* or of so-called *original decisions being quashed*, a very high percentage of the judgements typical of this perfidious judiciary, passed by the Austrian judiciary in recent years were so-called *political* mistrials, Reger said. We are faced in Austria today not only with an utterly rotten and *demoniacal* state but also with an utterly rotten and *demoniacal* judiciary, Reger said. The Austrian judiciary has had no credibility for many years now, it *operates in a despicable political manner, not independently,* as it should. To speak of an independent judiciary in Austria is to mock truth to its face, Reger said. Justice in Austria today is political justice, not independent justice. Today's Austrian judiciary has in fact become political and a public danger, Reger said, I know what I am talking about, he said. Justice today makes common cause with politics, Reger said, you only need to take a closer look some day at this Catholic National Socialist judiciary and study it with an open mind, Reger said. Austria today is, not only in Europe but worldwide, *the* country with the most so-called *miscarriages of justice,* that is what is so disastrous. You need only come into contact with the judiciary, and myself, as you know, have very often come into contact with the judiciary, and you will find that the Austrian judiciary is a dangerous Catholic National Socialist human grinding mill, kept in operation not by justice, as one would expect, but by injustice, and in which the most chaotic conditions prevail; there is no judiciary in Europe that is more chaotic than the Austrian, none that is more corrupt, none that is more of a public danger or more perfidious, Reger said, it is not the accidents of stupidity but the deliberate intentions of political baseness that govern the Catholic National Socialist Austrian judiciary today, Reger said. If you are taken to court in Austria you are at the mercy of a through and through chaotic Catholic National Socialist judiciary which turns the truth and facts upside down, Reger said. Austrian justice is not just arbitrariness but a perfidious machine for grinding human beings, Reger said, a machine in which justice is crushed between the absurd millstones of injustice. And as for culture in this country, all it does is turn our stomachs. As far as so-called *old art* is concerned, it is stale and washed out and sold out and has long forfeited any claim to our attention, you know that as well as I do, and as far as so-called contemporary art is concerned, it is *not worth a rap*, as the saying goes. Austrian contemporary art is so cheap it does not even deserve our blushes, Reger said. For decades now Austrian artists have produced nothing but kitschy rubbish, which indeed, if I had my way, would end up on the rubbish heap. The painters paint rubbish, the composers compose rubbish, the writers write rubbish, he said. The greatest rubbish is produced by the Austrian sculptors, Reger said. The Austrian sculptors produce the greatest rubbish and earn recognition for it, Reger said, that is typical of this stupid age. Today's Austrian composers are altogether only *petit-bourgeois* tone idiots whose concert-hall rubbish stinks to high heaven. And the Austrian writers have altogether nothing to say and cannot even write down that nothing they have to say. None of these present-day Austrian writers can write, they fill their pockets with a revoltingly sentimental epigone literature, Reger said, wherever they write they only write rubbish, they write Styrian and Salzburgian and Carinthian and Burgenlandish and Lower Austrian and Upper Austrian and Tyrolian and Vorarlbergian rubbish and they shovel that rubbish shamelessly and fame-hungrily between the covers of their books, Reger said. They sit in Viennese municipal flats or on Carinthian converted deserted smallholdings or in Styrian backyards, writing rubbish, that epigone, stinking, mindless and brainless Austrian writers' rubbish, Reger said, in *which the pathetic stupidity of these people stinks to high heaven*, Reger said. Their books are nothing but the rubbish of two or even three generations who never learned how to write because they never learned how to think, all these writers write totally brainless and sham-philosophical and sham-homeland epigone rubbish, Reger said. All these books by these more or less nauseatingly state-opportunist writers are *nothing but cribbed books*, Reger said, *every line in them is stolen, every word is pilfered.* For decades these people have written nothing but mindless literature written only out of a craving for admiration and likewise only published out of a craving for admiration, Reger said. They type their abysmal stupidity into their machines and for that abysmal insipid stupidity they collect all kinds of prizes, Reger said. Why, even Stifter was a great figure, Reger said, if I compare Stifter to all those Austrian dimwits who write today. Sham philosophy and sham homeland, at present greatly in vogue, is what the rubbish of those people is all about, Reger said, people incapable of a single idea of their own. The proper place for these people's books is not the bookshops but straight away the rubbish heap, Reger said. Just as the proper place for all present-day Austrian art is the rubbish heap. For what else is given at the Opera but rubbish, what else at the *Musikverein* but rubbish, and what else are the products of those brutal common proletarian men of violence with their chisels, who with positively overbearing impertinence call themselves sculptors, but marble and granite rubbish! It is frightful, for half a century nothing but this depressing mediocrity, Reger said. If Austria at least were a madhouse, but it is an infirmary, he said. The old have nothing to say, Reger said, but the young have even less to say, that is today's state of affairs. And of course all these art-producing people are too well off, he said. All these people are stuffed full of scholarships and of prizes and every other moment there is an honorary doctorate here and an honorary doctorate there and a pin of honour here and a pin of honour there and every other moment they sit next to one minister and shortly afterwards next to another and today they are with the Federal Chancellor and tomorrow with the Speaker of Parliament and today they sit in the socialist trade union hall and tomorrow in the Catholic working man's educational centre and let themselves be fêted and kept. These present artists are not only so mendacious in their so-called works, they are just as mendacious in their lives, Reger said. Mendacious work continually alternates for them with mendacious living, what they write is lies and what they live is lies, Reger said. And then these writers go on so-called *reading tours*, travelling in one way and another through the whole of Germany and through the whole of Austria and through the whole of Switzerland and they do not miss out even the most dull-witted backwoods dump for reading their rubbish and getting themselves fêted and they allow their pockets to be stuffed full of marks and of schillings and of francs, Reger said. There is nothing more distasteful than a so-called *poet's reading*, Reger said, there is hardly anything I detest more, but none of these people see anything wrong in reading their rubbish everywhere. Not a single person is basically interested in what these people have scavenged on their literary marauding expeditions, but they read it all the same, they get up on the stage and read it and they bow to every half-witted town councillor and to every dull-witted village mayor and to every jackanapes of a professor of German, Reger said. They read their rubbish from Flensburg down to Bolzano and let themselves be kept in the most brazen manner. There is nothing more intolerable for me than a so-called poet's reading, Reger said, it is repulsive to sit down and read one's own rubbish, because that is all those people do read – just rubbish. While they are still fairly young you can stretch a point, but once they are older, once they are in their fifties and beyond, it is just nauseating. But it is mainly these older writers, Reger said, who read everywhere and who climb up on every platform and who sit down at every table in order to present their poetic rubbish or their dull-witted senile prose, Reger said. Even if their dentures can no longer retain any of their mendacious words in their oral cavity, they still mount the platform of never mind what municipal hall and read their charlatanist nonsense, Reger said. A singer singing songs is insufferable enough, but a writer reciting his own products is a lot more insufferable still, Reger said. A writer stepping on to a public platform in order to read his opportunist rubbish, even if it is in Saint Paul's Church in Frankfurt, is a pitiful fairground ham, Reger said. Germany and Austria are swarming with such opportunist fairground hams, Reger said. Oh yes, he said, the logical conclusion would invariably be total despair *about everything*. But I am resisting this total despair *about everything*, Reger said. I am now eighty-two and I am resisting this total despair *about everything* tooth and nail, Reger said. In this world and in this age, he said, where anything is possible nothing will soon be possible. Irrsigler appeared and Reger nodded to him as if to say, you are better off than I am, and Irrsigler turned and disappeared again. Reger was supporting himself on his stick locked between his knees when he said: just reflect, Atzbacher, what it means to have the ambition to compose the longest-playing symphony in the history of music. No one else would have conceived such a nonsensical idea except Mahler. Some people say Mahler was the last great Austrian composer, that is ridiculous. A man who, in full control of his mind, has fifty strings fiddling away only to outdo Wagner is ridiculous. Austrian music reached its absolute low with Mahler, Reger said. Purest kitsch, generating mass hysteria, just as Klimt, he said. Schiele is the more important painter.

Nowadays even a poor Klimt kitsch painting costs several million pounds, Reger said, that is distasteful. Schiele is not kitsch, but of course Schiele is not a really great painter either. In this century there have been several Austrian painters of Schiele's quality, but, with the exception of Kokoschka, not a single really important one, a really great one, as it were. On the other hand, we have to admit that we cannot know what really great painting is. After all, here at the Kunsthistorisches Museum, we have instances of so-called great painting by the hundred, Reger said, but as time goes on they no longer seem to us to be great, no longer *so* important, because we have studied them too thoroughly. Anything we study thoroughly loses value for us, Reger said. We should therefore avoid studying anything *thoroughly*. But we cannot help studying everything thoroughly, that is our misfortune, by doing so we dissolve everything and ruin everything for us, indeed we have very nearly ruined everything for us already. A line of Goethe, Reger said; it is studied for so long by us that in the end it no longer seems quite as magnificent as at first, it gradually loses its value for us and what initially may have seemed to us the most magnificent line altogether ends up as an elemental disappointment. Anything we study thoroughly ultimately disappoints us. A mechanism of dissection and disintegration,

Reger said, that is a habit I acquired in my early years, without realizing that this was my misfortune. Even Shakespeare crumbles totally if we concern ourselves with him and *study* him for any length of time, his sentences get on your nerves, his characters disintegrate *before* the drama and ruin everything for us, he said. In the end we no longer take any pleasure in art, any more than in life, no matter how natural this may be, as progressively we have lost our naïveté and with it our stupidity. Yet in exchange we have only gained unhappiness. By now it has become absolutely impossible for me to read Goethe, Reger said, to listen to Mozart, to look at Leonardo or Giotto, I no longer have any prerequisites for that. Next week I shall again take Irrsigler to lunch at the *Astoria*, Reger said, while my wife was alive I used to go to the *Astoria* for lunch with her and with Irrsigler at least three times a year, I owe it to Irrsigler to continue those *Astoria* lunches, he said. We should not only use people like Irrsigler, we should also show them a kindness now and again. And the best way is for me to take Irrsigler to the *Astoria* for lunch. Of course I could take his family to the Prater from time to time, but I do not feel up to that, the Irrsigler children hang on to me like burrs and well-nigh tear the clothes off me with their effusiveness, he said. And the Prater is so distasteful to me, you know, the sight of all those drunken men and women cracking their cheap jokes in front of the shooting galleries and giving free rein to their horrid primitiveness, I feel soiled all over whenever I have gone to the Prater. But then the Prater today is no longer the Prater as it was in my childhood, the turbulent amusement park; the Prater today is a distasteful assembly of vulgar people, an assembly of criminal types. The whole Prater reeks of beer and crime and we encounter in it nothing but the brutality and the brazen feeble-mindedness of vulgar snotty Viennesedom. Not a day passes without a murder in the Prater being in the papers, every day at least one, usually several, rapes in the Prater. In my childhood the Prater always was a joyous day out and in spring there really was a perfume of lilac and chestnuts there. Today proletarian perversity stinks to high heaven. The Prater, this most charming of all inventions for amusement, is now nothing but a common fairground of vulgarity. Ah, if the Prater were still as it was in my childhood, Reger said, I would go there with the Irrsigler family, but as it is I do not go there, I cannot afford to; if I went to the Prater with the Irrsigler family I should be wrecked for weeks to come. My mother was still driven to the Prater with her parents in the carriage and would run along the Prater Avenue in a floating silk dress. Such pictures are history, Reger said, all that is long past. Today you are lucky if you are not shot in the back in the Prater, Reger said, or stabbed in the heart, or at the least have your wallet lifted from your jacket. The present age is an utterly brutalized age. Taking the Irrsigler children to the Prater is something I have done only once, never again. They hung on me like burrs and tore the clothes off me and demanded every other moment that I took them on the ghost train or on the automatic merry-go-round. It made me feel quite sick, Reger said. Needless to say, I have nothing against the Irrsigler children, Reger said, but they are too much for me. Irrsigler on his own is all right, but the whole Irrsigler family, that is impossible. With Irrsigler at the Astoria, at my corner table looking out at the deserted May-sedergasse, that is all right, but with the Irrsigler family to the Prater, that is impossible. Each time I invent a new excuse in order not to have to go to the Prater with the Irrsigler family. A visit to the Prater with the Irrsigler family seems to me like a visit to hell. I also cannot bear the voice of Frau Irrsigler, Reger said, I cannot bear that voice. The Irrsigler children also have basically frightful voices, it does not bear thinking about those voices growing up, he said. Such a quiet pleasant person as Irrsigler and such a loud-voiced woman as the Irrsigler woman and such loud-voiced children as the Irrsigler children. On one occasion Irrsigler suggested that I should make a trip into the countryside with him and his family. That, too, I declined and I have been writhing for years to escape just such a *rural excursion* with the Irrsigler family. Imagine me hiking through the countryside with the Irrsigler family, quite possibly the Irrsigler children would even start singing. That I could not stand: the Irrsigler children expecting me to march through the woods of the surroundings of Vienna with them, the Irrsigler woman in front and Irrsigler at the rear and alongside me, holding hands if they had their way, the Irrsigler children. And then the Irrsigler family might possibly expect me to join in their singsong. Simple people have this urge towards nature, an urge towards the open spaces, I have never had that urge, Reger said. There is nothing more ghastly that could happen to me than hiking with the Irrsigler family through the surroundings of Vienna and then perhaps even to stop at an inn garden. I was nauseated at the thought of the Irrsigler family eating fried schnitzels in my presence and filling their bellies with wine and beer and apple juice at my expense. Lunching with Irrsigler at the Astoria is something I enjoy too, I do not need any pretence for that, lunching with Irrsigler at the *Astoria*, three times a year, a glass of wine with it, Reger said, that is all right, anything else is not. The Prater is absolutely impossible and the surroundings of Vienna are absolutely impossible.

If Irrsigler had even a spark of musicality in him, Reger said, I would take him along to a concert now and again or I would simply let him have my press tickets, but Irrsigler has not the slightest feeling for music, he suffers agonies when he has to listen to music. Anybody else, even if it is agony to him, will take his seat in the Musikverein in the third or fourth row to listen to Beethoven's Fifth, because there, more than anywhere else, everything favours human vanity; not so Irrsigler, he has always declined to go to the Musikverein and always with the simple statement: I *don't like music, Herr Reger*, Reger said. For three years the Irrsigler family has been waiting for me to go to the Prater with them, Reger said, and one time I have a headache and another time I have a sore throat and yet another time I am snowed under with work and another still I have to catch up on my correspondence and each time I find it distasteful to have to say these things. Irrsigler knows perfectly well why I do not go to the Prater with his family, I have not told him why but then Irrsigler is no fool, Reger said. At the *Astoria* he always orders the same silverside of beef because I always order the same silverside of beef. He waits until I have ordered my silverside of beef and then orders silverside of beef for himself, Reger said. But whereas I only drink mineral water, Irrsigler takes a glass of wine with his silverside of beef. The silverside at the *Astoria* is not always first-class, but I quite simply prefer it to anything else at the *Astoria*. Irrsigler eats slowly, that is the unusual thing about him. I myself eat my silverside of beef so slowly that I think I must be eating even more slowly than Irrsigler, but Irrsigler, even though I eat my silverside of beef as slowly as possible, eats his a lot more slowly still. Irrsigler, I said to him at the *Astoria* last time, I owe you so much, probably everything, naturally he did not understand. After the death of my wife I was suddenly all alone, true I had a lot of people but not really any individual and I certainly did not wish to bother *you* in my dreadful state. For six months I avoided all contact with people, if only because I wished to escape from their frightful enquiries, *people always ask those dreadful questions about someone's death in such an unashamed manner* and at every opportunity; that is what I wished to escape, and so I only had Irrsigler. And for nearly six months after my wife's death I did not come to the Kunsthistorisches Museum, it is only for the past six months that I have been coming here again, and initially of course not every other day as had been my habit but once a week at the most. But now, for the past six months I have again come to the Kunst- historisches Museum every other day. Irrsigler, because he never asked anything, was the only possible person, Reger said. I always reflect, should I take Irrsigler *to the Astoria* or *to the Imperial*, anyway to one of the very top restaurants, but at the *Imperial* he does not feel as comfortable as at the *Astoria*, a person like Irrsigler cannot bear the absolute magnificence of the *Imperial*, Reger said. And the *Astoria* is also a lot more discreet. In this way I hope, from time to time, to discharge my gratitude to Irrsigler, who is so important to me, Reger said. Irrsigler has the agreeable quality of being a good listener, moreover of being a good listener in an entirely unpresuming way. Whereas Irrsigler is the most pleasant person to me, the Irrsigler family as a whole are the most unpleasant. How does a person like Irrsigler, Reger asked, come to have a wife as the Irrsigler woman with her shrill voice and her hen-like walk? We often ask ourselves how people who are such complete opposites come together, Reger said. A woman with a hysterical animal voice and with a hen-like walk and a man like Irrsigler who is so balanced and so agreeable. And the Irrsigler children, of course, in virtually everything are taking after their mother and in virtually nothing after their father. Each more *mal-réussi* than the other, Reger said. The Irrsigler children are all *mal-réussis*, Reger said, *but of course the parents believe they have réussis children, all parents believe that.* It is a positively frightening thought what may become of these Irrsigler children one day, Reger said, when I see these Irrsigler children then I see, even today, by no means at least average but far below-average human beings with, at best, a dichotomous character. I am always reminded, Reger said, of *the concept of the stupid brood*, that is what is so unpleasant about the Irrsigler family. Such an excellent man and such a fine character and such an ill-bred family. All this is quite commonplace, Reger said. The Austrians, being congenital opportunists, are cringers, he now said, and they live by cover-ups and forgetting. There is no political atrocity, no matter how great, that is not forgotten after a week, no crime, no matter how great. The Austrians are positively congenital *coverers-up* of crimes, Reger said, the Austrians will cover up any crime, even the vilest, because they are, as I have said, congenital opportunist cringers. For decades our ministers have committed ghastly crimes, yet these opportunist cringers cover up for them. For decades these ministers have committed *murderous* frauds, yet these cringers cover up for them. For decades these unscrupulous Austrian ministers have lied to the Austrians and cheated them and yet these cringers cover up for them. It is a real miracle if, now and again, one of those criminal and fraudulent ministers is kicked out, Reger said, because he is accused of serious crimes committed for decades, yet a week later the whole affair is forgotten because the cringers have forgotten the affair. A twenty-schilling thief is prosecuted by our justice and locked up, but a de-frauder of millions and billions, when of ministerial rank, is at best chased out with a huge pension and instantly forgotten, Reger said. It really is a miracle, Reger continued, that a minister has just been booted out again, but, mind you, no sooner was he sacked and kicked out and no sooner had the papers called him a billion-schilling swindler and a major criminal who should be put on trial than he will be forgotten in perpetuity by those selfsame papers and hence also by the entire public. Although the minister should be charged and put on trial and locked up, in accordance with his crime, if I may say so *for life*, he enjoys his fat pension in his villa on the Kahlenberg and no one dreams any longer of interfering with him. He lives, as the saying goes, *on the fat of the land* as a retired minister and when one day he dies he is even given a state funeral and a grave of honour at the Central Cemetery, Reger said, alongside his predeceased ministerial colleagues who were the same kind of criminals as he. Austrians are congenital coverers-up and forgetters where the atrocities and crimes of ministers and other governing figures are concerned, Reger said. Austrians spend all their lives cringing and covering up the worst atrocities and crimes in order to survive themselves, that is the truth, Reger said. The papers merely record and accuse and of course magnify, but they immediately annul everything opportunistically and forget opportunistically. The papers are the discoverers and the agitators and at the same time the coverers-up and the whitewashers and oppressors where political atrocities and crimes are concerned, Reger said. Just recall how the papers execrated the now retired minister and levelled the most serious charges against him and, as the saying goes, *finished* him and forced the Federal Chancellor to dismiss him, and no sooner had the Federal Chancellor dismissed this minister than the papers forget all about the minister and with him the atrocities and crimes which he in fact committed, Reger said. Austrian justice is a justice made compliant by the Austrian politicians, Reger said, anything else is a lie. The fact that this affair was hushed up not only by the government but also by the papers preys on my mind, Reger said. But if you are an Austrian things would have been preying on your mind for years, because over these past few years not a day has passed without a political scandal and political corruption has assumed a scale that would have been inconceivable a few years ago, Reger said. Whatever my mind may be occupied with, these political scandals are continually on my mind, disturbing it. Do what I like, these political scandals are on my mind, Reger said, whatever I am engaged in, these political scandals are on my mind,

Reger said. Whenever we open our paper we have another political scandal, Reger said, every day a new scandal involving politicians of this *state, by now mutilated beyond recognition*, politicians who abused their office, who made common cause with crime. When you open your paper you think you are living in a state where political atrocities and political criminality have become a daily occurrence. Initially I told myself I would not let myself get worked up because this state today is thoroughly and utterly beyond discussion, but all of a sudden I find it quite impossible *not* to get worked up in this horrid and daily more horrendous state; when you open your paper in the morning you quite automatically get worked up about the atrocities and the crimes of our politicians. Quite automatically you gain the impression that all politicians are criminal types and are fundamentally criminal and a pack of swine, Reger said. In consequence I have lately broken myself of the habit of reading the paper in the morning, as had been my custom for decades, it is enough for me to open it in the afternoon. If a newspaper reader opens his paper first thing in the morning he makes himself sick first thing in the morning and for the rest of the day and even for the subsequent night, Reger said, because he is confronted with an ever bigger political scandal, with ever bigger political corruption, Reger said. The newspaper reader in this country has for years read nothing but scandal in his paper, on the first three pages the political scandal and on the following pages the rest; but whatever he does all he reads about is scandal because the Austrian papers now write about nothing but scandal and corruption, about nothing else. The Austrian papers have reached such a low level that this too is a scandal, Reger said, there are no lower or baser or more repugnant papers in the world than the Austrian papers, but these Austrian papers are of necessity so hideous and so base because Austrian society, above all Austrian political society, and this state are all so hideous and so base. Never before has there been such a hideous or base society in this country with such a hideous and base state, Reger said, but no one in this state and in this country regards this as a disgrace, no one really rebels against it, Reger said. Austrians have always accepted everything, no matter what it was, even though it was the worst atrocity and the greatest infamy, even if it was the most monstrous of all monstrosities, Reger said. Austrians are anything but revolutionaries because they are no fanatics of truth at all, Austrians have for centuries lived with lies and got used to it, Reger said, Austrians have for centuries been wedded to lies, to every lie, Reger said, but most deeply and most of all to the lies of the state. Austrians live their common and base Austrian lives with the lies of the state, without giving them another thought, Reger said, that is what is so repulsive about them. Your so-called charming Austrian is an insidious and opportunist setter of traps, Reger said, who always and everywhere sets his opportunist traps, the so-called charming Austrian is a master of the most infamous infamy, beneath his so-called charm he is the most infamous and shameless and ruthless person and *for this very reason* the most mendacious, Reger said. Although I have been a fanatical reader of newspapers all my life, Reger said, I now find it well-nigh unbearable to open a paper because they are only full of scandals. But then the papers reflect the society they report on, Reger said. You may search for a whole year and you will not find a single intelligent sentence in any of these filthy rags, Reger said. But why am I telling you all this when you are just as familiar with everything Austrian, Reger said. I woke up this morning and thought of the ministerial scandal and I cannot get that ministerial scandal out of my mind, that is the tragedy of my mind, Reger said, that I cannot get these scandals, and above all these political scandals, out of my mind, these scandals are eating ever more deeply into my mind, that is the tragedy. I tell myself that I must get all these scandals and atrocities out of my mind and yet these atrocities and scandals are eating ever more deeply into my mind. But of course I find it soothing to talk to you about all these things and more especially about these political atrocities and scandals, every morning I think how fortunate for me to have the Ambassador in order to be able to talk to you and of course not only about the scandals and the atrocities, because naturally there are other things as well, more cheerful ones, such as music, Reger said. So long as I still feel like talking about the *Tempest Sonata* or about the Art of the Fugue I am not giving up, Reger said. Music saves me time and again, the fact that music is still alive within me, and it still is as alive in me as on the day I was born, Reger said. To be saved anew by music every morning, from all the atrocities and hideousnesses, he said, that is it; to be made once more into a thinking and feeling individual by music, you understand, he said. Ah yes, Reger said, even if we curse it at times, even if at times it seems to us entirely superfluous and even if we have to say it is not worth anything, this art, yet when we look on these pictures here, these so-called old masters, though they have very often, and increasingly so over the years, seemed pointless and useless, nothing but helpless attempts to establish themselves artistically on the surface of the earth, it is nothing else but just this cursed and damned and often (to the point of vomiting) revolting and embarrassing art that saves such as ourselves, Reger said. The Austrian has always been a clever person, Reger said, and he is profoundly aware of being that. That is the cause of all his distastefulness, of his weakness of character, because more than from any other distastefulness the Austrian suffers from a weak character. But that also makes him a lot more interesting than all others, Reger said. The Austrian is actually the most interesting type of all European types, because he has everything of every other European type plus his own weakness of character on top. That is what is so fascinating about the Austrian, Reger said, that all the qualities of all the others are present in him from birth and his own weakness of character on top. If we spend all our lives in Austria we do not see the Austrian as he really is, but if, after a prolonged absence such as mine in London, we return to Austria we see him clearly and he cannot pretend to us. The Austrian is a genius at pretending, the greatest genius at play-acting altogether, Reger said, he pretends to be everything without ever being any of it in fact, that is his most prominent characteristic. The Austrian is popular throughout the world, at least he is to this day, and the whole world has, so to speak, always been fooled simply because he is *the most interesting European type*, yet at the same time he is always also *the most dangerous*. The Austrian is very probably the most dangerous type altogether, more dangerous than the German, more dangerous than any other European, the Austrian is definitely the most dangerous political type, this has been demonstrated by history, and time and again this has brought the greatest misfortune upon Europe and indeed very often upon the whole world. No matter how interesting or unique we may find the Austrian, who invariably is a common Nazi or a stupid Catholic, we must not allow him to seize the political rudder, Reger said, because an Austrian at the rudder always and inescapably steers everything into a total abyss. A sleepless night and exasperation over these everlasting political scandals, Reger then said. Yes, I thought first thing in the morning, you will be meeting Atzbacher at the Kunsthistorisches Museum to put a proposal to him, and you know perfectly well that you will be putting a totally nonsensical proposal to him, but you will put the proposal to him. A ludicrous matter and nevertheless a monstrous one, Reger said. For two months after the death of his wife Reger did not leave his flat on the Singerstrasse and for six months after the death of his wife he did not meet a single person. For these six months he was being looked after by his *vulgar and dreadful* housekeeper and not once did he go to the Kunsthistorisches Museum, where for decades he had been every other

day with his wife, I now reflect. His housekeeper
cooked for him and washed his clothes, even though
doing *everything in an outrageously slovenly manner*,
Reger said time and again, but at least he did not go
to seed completely. A person suddenly left alone
goes to seed very rapidly, Reger himself said, for
months I ate nothing but semolina pudding, Reger said,
because with my unrepaired dentures I could no longer
eat any meat or even any vegetables. The Singerstrasse
flat has become silent as the grave and empty, this was
Reger's own description of the state of affairs when
I met him at the Ambassador for the first time after
his wife's death, haggard, pale, supporting himself on
his stick nearly all the time, his laces undone and his
winter longjohns slipping out from his trouser legs.
We do not wish to go on living when we have lost the
person closest to us, he said to me at the Ambassador
then, but we have to go on living, we do not kill
ourselves because we are too cowardly for that, we
promise by the open grave that we shall soon follow
and then, six months later, we are still alive and we
have a horror of ourselves, Reger said to me at the
Ambassador then. His wife was eighty-seven, but
she could certainly have lived well into her hundreds
had she not had that fall, Reger said to me at the
Ambassador then. The city of Vienna and the Austrian
state and the Catholic Church, Reger said to me at

the Ambassador then, are responsible for her death, because if the city of Vienna, which owns the approach to the Kunsthistorisches Museum, had gritted the approach to the Kunsthistorisches Museum my wife would not have had a fall, and if the Kunsthistorisches Museum, which belongs to the state, had notified the ambulance service at once and not half an hour later, my wife would have got to the Merciful Brethren Hospital sooner than an hour after her fall, or if the surgeons at the Merciful Brethren Hospital, which belongs to the Catholic Church, had not bungled the operation, my wife would not have died, Reger said to me at the Ambassador then. The city of Vienna and the Austrian state and the Catholic Church are responsible for the death of my wife, Reger said at the Ambassador, I now reflected while sitting next to him on the Bordone Room settee. The city of Vienna fails to grit the approach to the Kunsthistorisches Museum on a day when it is icy and the Kunsthistorisches Museum notifies the ambulance service only after repeated requests and finally the surgeons at the Merciful Brethren Hospital bungle the operation and in the end my wife is dead, Reger said at the Ambassador. We lose the person we have loved most devotedly of all people solely through the negligence of the city of Vienna and through the negligence of the Austrian state and through the negligence of the

Catholic Church, Reger said at the Ambassador then. We lose the person most important to us because the city and the state and the Church have acted negligently, Reger said at the Ambassador then. The person with whom we have shared our life for nearly forty years, in the most natural way and with respect and love, dies because the city and the state and the Church have acted negligently and infamously, Reger said at the Ambassador then. We are suddenly left alone by the one person whom, basically, we had, because the city and the state and the Church have acted thoughtlessly and irresponsibly, Reger said at the Ambassador then. All of a sudden we are cut off from the person to whom we owe *basically everything* and who in fact gave us everything, Reger said at the Ambassador then. We are suddenly alone in our flat without the person who has kept us alive with the greatest care for some decades, simply because city and state and Catholic Church have committed the crime of negligence, Reger said at the Ambassador then. We stand by the open grave of the person whom we have never been able to imagine living without, Reger said at the Ambassador then. The city of Vienna and the Austrian state and the Catholic Church are responsible for my being alone now and for my having to be alone as long as I live, Reger said at the Ambassador then. The person who had always been in good health and who had every conceivable virtue of an intelligent *and* female person and who in fact had been the most loving person in my life dies and leaves me only because the city of Vienna does not grit the approach to the Kunsthistorisches Museum, only because the Kunsthistorisches Museum, which belongs to the state, does not notify the ambulance service in time and because the surgeons at the, Merciful Brethren Hospital bungle the operation, Reger said at the Ambassador then. My wife might have lived into her hundreds, I am convinced of it, if the city of Vienna had gritted the approach to the Kunsthistorisches Museum, Reger said at the Ambassador then. And she would certainly still be alive if the Kunsthistorisches, Museum had notified the ambulance service in time and if the surgeons at the Merciful Brethren Hospital had not bungled the operation. Strictly speaking I should not have entered the Kunsthistorisches Museum again, Reger said, having entered it again seven months after the death of his wife. Now the approach to the Kunsthistorisches Museum is gritted, now that my wife is dead, Reger said. And why did they have to take my wife to the Merciful Brethren Hospital, of all places, to a hospital of which I have never heard a good word, Reger said. All these hospitals with the word *merciful* in their title are utterly distasteful to me, Reger said. The word *merciful* is abused more than almost any other word, Reger said. The merciful hospitals are the most merciless I know, Reger said, in them, as a rule, reigns only avarice and a lack of skill, quite apart from that utterly infamous and base sham-religiosity, Reger said at the Ambassador then. Now I have only the Ambassador left, Reger said at the Ambassador then, this corner to which I have become used over the decades. I have two locations to which I can escape when I no longer know where to turn, Reger said at the Ambassador then, this corner here at the Ambassador and the settee at the Kunsthistorisches Museum. But sitting all alone in this corner here at the Ambassador is also terrible, Reger said at the Ambassador then. Sitting here with my wife used to be one of my favourite occupations, not sitting here on my own, not here on my own, my dear Atzbacher, Reger said at the Ambassador then, and sitting on my own on the Bordone Room settee at the Kunsthistorisches Museum is also terrible, when I have sat on it with my wife for over three decades. When I walk through the city of Vienna I keep thinking that the city of Vienna is responsible for the death of my wife and that the Austrian state is responsible for her death and that the Catholic Church is responsible for her death, no matter where I go, I cannot get this idea out of my mind, Reger said. A crime has been committed against me, a municipal-governmental-Catholic-ecclesiastical atrocity that I can do nothing about, that is the worst of it, Reger said. Basically, Reger said at the Ambassador then, I also died at the moment my wife died. The truth is that I feel like a dead man, like a dead man who has to go on living. That is my problem, Reger said at the Ambassador then. The flat is empty and deserted, Reger said several times at the Ambassador then. In all those twenty years I have only twice been to the Regers' flat on the Singerstrasse, a ten- or twelve-room flat in a building of the turn of the century, which now, after the death of Reger's wife, belongs to Reger. Filled with the furniture of his wife's family, the Regers' flat on the Singerstrasse is a fine example of a so-called *art nouveau* flat, with actually masses of Klimts and Schieles and Gerstls and Kokoschkas hanging on the walls, *all of them pictures my wife valued greatly*, as Reger said on one occasion, *but which always profoundly repelled me*. Every single room in the Regers' Singerstrasse flat had been transformed into a real work of art about the turn of the century *by a famous Slovak artist in wood, I do not really believe that there is another flat in Vienna, where Slovak woodwork art has been applied with such skill or with such very high demands of craftsmanship or so totally successfully*, dear Atzbacher. Reger himself, as he keeps saying, does not in the least appreciate the so-called

art nouveau style, he detests it, *because the whole of
the art nouveau style is nothing but kitsch* but, as he kept
saying, he enjoyed *the cosiness of the Singerstrasse flat*
of his wife, *the réussis proportions of all the rooms* in it,
above all the dimensions of his study, but since, as
mentioned before, he had no taste whatever for the
so-called *art nouveau* style, he always appreciated only
the comfort of the Singerstrasse flat, which had always
been *ideal for the two of us*, but not its furnishings. On
my first visit to the Regers' Singerstrasse flat, when
Reger received me because his wife had gone to
Prague, he conducted me briefly through the whole
flat, *this then is where I exist*, he said then, *you see, here
in these rooms, which suit me eminently, even though this
hideous uncomfortable furniture is not to my taste at all.*
All this is my wife's taste, not mine, Reger said then,
and when I looked at the paintings on the walls he,
would say time and again, *ah yes, this I believe is a
Schiele, ah yes, this I believe is a Klimt, ah yes, this I believe
is a Kokoschka. Turn-of-the-century painting is nothing
but kitsch and has no appeal for me*, he said several times,
*whereas my wife has always been attracted by it, even if
not actually fascinated, but attracted that is the right
expression*, Reger said. *Schiele perhaps, but not Klimt;
Kokoschka yes, Gerstl no*, these were his observations.
Reputedly Loos, *reputedly* Hoffmann, he said, when I said
surely this table was by Adolf Loos, surely this chair

was by Josef Hoffmann. You know, Reger said, I have always been repelled by things which are fashionable at the moment, and Loos and Hoffmann are so fashionable now that *quite naturally I am repelled by them.* And Schiele and Klimt, those kitsch-mongers, are the height of fashion today, which is why Klimt and Schiele basically so repel me. People nowadays listen predominantly to Webern and Schoenberg and Berg and those who ape them, and also to Mahler, that repels me. Anything in fashion has always repelled me. Most probably I also suffer from what I call *art selfishness:* where art is concerned I wish to have everything for myself alone, I want to possess my Schopenhauer for myself, my Pascal, my Novalis and my fervently loved Gogol, *I alone* want to possess these art products, these inspired artistic eccentricities, *I alone* want to possess Michelangelo, Renoir, Goya, he said, I can scarcely bear the thought that someone else, apart from me, possesses and enjoys the products of these geniuses, the very idea is unbearable to me that, apart from me, another person even appreciates Janáček, or Martinů or Schopenhauer or Descartes, I find this almost unbearable, *I want to be the only one, that of course is a dreadful attitude,* Reger said then. I *am a possessive thinker,* Reger said then. I *am a possessive thinker,* Reger said in his flat then. *I should like to think that Goya painted only for me, that Gogol and*

Goethe wrote only for me, that Bach composed only for me.
As this is a fallacy and moreover a piece of abysmal
meanness I am basically always unhappy, I am sure
you understand, Reger said then. Even though this is
nonsense, Reger said then, when I read a book I still
have the feeling and the belief that the book was
written for me alone, when I view a picture I have the
feeling and the belief that it was painted only for me,
or that the composition I hear was composed only
for me. Naturally I read myself and listen and view
myself into a great error, but I do so with very great
enjoyment, Reger said then. Here in this chair, Reger
said to me then, pointing to what he called a *hideous
Loos chair, which Loos incidentally designed in Brussels
and had manufactured in Brussels*, I introduced my wife
to the Art of the Fugue thirty years ago. The *hideous
Loos chair* still stands in the same spot. And here, on
this *hideous Loos settee* – he had invited me to sit down
on this *hideous Loos settee* which stood before a window
looking out on to the Singerstrasse – I read Wieland
to my wife for a whole year, *Wieland, that great but
underrated figure in German literature, Wieland whom
Goethe winkled out of Weimar, with Schiller playing a
distasteful part in it*, Reger, said; after a year my wife
was a *Wieland expert, after a single year!* Reger exclaimed
then. And here on this *Loos footstool, which is as uncomfortable as it is hideous*, reputedly this footstool was

also designed by *that unbearably grand-gesture man Loos*, my wife would sit and between one and two every morning, during sixty-six and sixty-seven, read me the whole of Kant. To start with I had the greatest difficulty in introducing my wife to the world of literature and of philosophy and of music, Reger said then. It is obvious, surely, that literature is not conceivable without philosophy or the other way round, or philosophy without music or literature without music or the other way round, he said, it took years before my wife understood this, Reger said at the Singerstrasse flat then. I had to start from the very beginning with my wife, even though, if only through her origins, she was correspondingly highly educated when I met her. *At first I thought that living together would be impossible, but then it was possible after all*, Reger said, *because my wife subordinated herself, naturally*, because that was the prerequisite of our living together, which eventually I was able to describe as an ideal living together. A woman such as my wife only experiences difficulty in learning during the first few years of such a schooling, thereafter she learns ever more easily, Reger said. On this *uncomfortable and hideous Loos footstool* my wife, in a manner of speaking, saw the light of philosophy, Reger said at the Singerstrasse flat then. For years we pursue the wrong road of illuminating a person before, from one moment to the next, we *perceive* the correct one, from then on everything moves very quickly, from then on my wife comprehended everything very quickly, but of course I could have continued to work on her for certainly some years if not decades, Reger said at the Singerstrasse flat then. We take a wife and we do not know why we have taken her, surely not just so she should be a nuisance to us with her everlasting domestic fussing, in what is simply her feminine way, Reger said at the Singerstrasse flat then, surely we take her because we wish to acquaint her with the true value of life, to instruct her on what life can be *if conducted intellectually.* Of course we must not make the mistake of drilling intellectuality into the head of such a woman, as I had attempted initially and was naturally bound to fail, here too it is circumspection that leads to results, Reger said at the Singerstrasse flat then. Anything my wife had loved before we met she stopped loving once I had enlightened her, except for that *art nouveau* hysteria, this so-called *art-nouveau*, this repulsive kitsch art, this nauseating *art-nouveau* aberration of taste: there I stood no chance. I did of course succeed in gradually curing her of false, which means worthless, literature and of false and worthless music, Reger said, and I introduced her to *essential sections of world philosophy.* The female head is the most obstinate, Reger said at the Singerstrasse flat then, we believe it to be accessible whereas in fact it is inaccessible. Before I married my wife she went on a lot of nonsensical journeys, Reger said then, which subsequently she no longer did, she simply had, as have most women nowadays, a travel mania, one place today, another tomorrow, that is their slogan yet basically they experience nothing, they see nothing, they bring back with them nothing but an empty purse. After our wedding my wife made no more journeys, Reger said, only *those journeys of the mind*, on which I accompanied her, we travelled through Schopenhauer and through Nietzsche and through Descartes and through Montaigne and through Pascal, and always for several years, Reger said. Here, you see, Reger said at the Singerstrasse flat then while sitting down on a chair, a *hideous Otto Wagner chair*, on this *hideous Otto Wagner chair* my wife confessed to me that, although I had instructed her in Schleiermacher for a whole year, she had not understood Schleiermacher. As, however, in the course of that instruction on Schleiermacher I had taken a dislike to Schleiermacher myself so that suddenly I no longer had the slightest interest in Schleiermacher myself, I quite simply took note that she had not understood Schleiermacher and no longer concerned myself with Schleiermacher; in such a situation we must quite simply and quite ruthlessly brush aside, as the saying goes, any philosopher whom our wife fails to understand, as for instance Schleiermacher, and move on. I immediately embarked on an instruction in Herder, this we both found to be a relaxation, Reger said at the Singerstrasse flat then. After the death of my wife I considered moving out of our joint flat, but then I did not move out, quite simply because I am too old for a move. A move would be beyond my strength. Naturally, two rooms would be sufficient, Reger said, but when one can no longer move out of a flat one has to make do with ten or twelve, as in the case of the Singerstrasse flat. Everything in this flat reminds me of my wife, Reger said, no matter where I look, she is always standing here, sitting there, coming towards me from this room or that, it is terrible even though, at the same time, it is heart-rending, it is in fact heart-rending, Reger said. That time, on my first visit to the Singerstrasse flat, while his wife was still alive, he said to me while gazing down on to the Singerstrasse, you know, Atzbacher, there is nothing I fear more than finding myself suddenly left by my wife and alone, the most frightful thing that could happen to me would be her dying and leaving me alone. But my wife is in good health and will survive me by many years, Reger said then. When we love a person as tenderly as I do my wife we cannot imagine their death, we cannot even bear the thought of it, Reger said then. When I was at the Singerstrasse flat for the second time it was to collect an old volume of Spinoza which he had obtained for me at a more favourable price than normal, that is not through an official bookshop but *through an illegal dealer*, and as soon as I stepped into the Singerstrasse flat he made me sit down in the nearest chair, also a *hideous Loos chair*, and disappeared into his library, from where shortly afterwards he reappeared with a volume of Novalis maxims. I shall now read you Novalis maxims for an hour, he said to me, and, while I had to remain seated on the *hideous Loos chair*, he remained standing and for an actual hour read Novalis maxims to me. I have loved Novalis from the start, he said, when he had closed the book with the Novalis maxims after an hour, and I still love him today. Novalis is the poet whom I have loved all my life always in the same way and always with the same intensity, more than any other. As time went on the lot of them, more or less, invariably, got on my nerves, profoundly disappointed me, revealed themselves as nonsensical or as pointless or, just as often, ultimately insignificant and useless, but there was none of this in the case of Novalis. I never believed I could love a poet who was at the same time a philosopher, but I love Novalis, I have always loved him and at all times and I shall love him in the future too with the same sincerity with which I have always loved him, Reger said then. All philosophers age with time, not so Novalis, Reger said then. But it is surely strange that my wife never even had a liking for Novalis, not even a *liking*, whereas I have always *totally* loved Novalis. There were a great many things I was able to convince my wife about, in time, but not about Novalis, although Novalis is the one author she would have gained from most, he said. At first she refused to go to the Kunsthistorisches Museum with me, Reger now said, she resisted, so to speak, tooth and nail, but eventually she came here with me after all, with the same regularity as myself, and I am convinced that, if she had survived me instead of me surviving her, as is the case now, she would have come to the Kunsthistorisches Museum on her own again, without me, just as I am doing now, alone, without her. Reger again looked at the *White-Bearded Man* and said: forty years after the end of the war conditions in Austria have again reached their darkest moral low, that is what is so depressing. Such a beautiful country and such an utterly brutal and vile and self-destructive society. What is so appalling about it is that one can only be a perplexed spectator of the catastrophe and is unable to do anything about it, Reger said. Reger gazed at the *White-Bearded Man* and said: every other day I visit my wife's grave and I stand there by her grave for half an hour and I feel nothing. That is the strange thing, that I think of nothing but my wife more or less the whole time and when I stand there by her grave I feel nothing relating to her. I stand there and actually do not feel anything relating to her. Only when I walk away from the grave again do I once more experience the horror of her having left me. I always think I visit her grave in order to be particularly close to her, but when I am standing there by her grave I do not even feel anything relating to her. But I have made it a habit to visit my wife's grave every other day, the grave which one day will also be my own, Reger said. When I recall the ghastly circumstances connected with her funeral I still feel sick today. Time and again the printer printed the In Memoriam sheet, which I had ordered, wrongly, first too boldly, then too faintly, first with too many commas, then with too few, he said, each time I got him to show me the proof everything was wrong, it was enough to drive me to despair. At the peak of my despair I said to the printer that surely I had given him a very precise copy, except that the proofs never followed my copy and that everything was always wrong in the proofs. Whereupon the printer said to me that *he* knew how such an In Memoriam notice should be printed, *not I*, he knew how the text should be set, *not I*, *he* knew where the commas belonged, *not I*. But I did not give in and eventually I held in my hands the In Memoriam notice I wanted; but I had to go to the printing shop five times, Reger said, in order to get an In Memoriam notice the way I wanted it. Printers are conceited people who claim to be right even when they have long realized that they are not right. You must not tangle with printers, Reger said, they get bolshie at once and threaten to chuck everything unless you bow to their blinkered ideas. But I have never bowed to printers, Reger said. There was only a single sentence on the In Memoriam, Reger said, only the place and date of my wife's death, yet I had to go to the print shop five times and actually had to argue with the printer. My wife did not really want to have an In Memoriam notice, we had agreed on that, but nevertheless I had an In Memoriam printed, Reger said; however, I never posted off a single In Memoriam because suddenly, just as I was about to post them, it seemed nonsense to me to post the In Memoriam notices. I merely put a single brief sentence into the papers, simply that my wife had died, Reger said. People are terribly extravagant when someone dies, I kept everything as simple as humanly possible, Reger said, although of course I am not sure today that I did the right thing, I have continual doubts in that respect, these doubts have been assailing me every day since my wife's death, not one day without these doubts, that wears you down in the long run, Reger said. As for the estate, there was not the slightest problem, as she had appointed me in her will as, so to speak, her *sole heir*, just as in turn I appointed her my *sole heir* in my will. Such a death, no matter how painful, even if one believes it would choke one, also has its ridiculous side. The terrible, after all, is always ridiculous, Reger said. Basically my wife's funeral was not only a simple funeral but also a depressing one, Reger said. We hope for a simple funeral, with as few people as possible, Reger said, and find we have merely arranged a depressing one. We say: no music, we say: no speeches, and we think that will be the simplest and the easiest way for us to survive, and yet it depresses us, profoundly, Reger said. Only seven or eight people, really only the very closest, if possible no relatives and only the very closest, that is what we think, and then what we get is just these very closest only, whom moreover we have told, *no flowers, nothing*, and then everything turns out very depressing. We walk behind the coffin and everything is depressing. Everything happens very quickly, it hardly takes three-quarters of an hour and it depresses us and we believe that it took an eternity, Reger said. I visit my wife's grave and I feel absolutely nothing. At home to this day I still feel like howling at least once every day, he said, believe it or not, but by my wife's grave I feel nothing at all. I stand there, tearing up blades of grass, making those nervous ridiculous tearing movements which I know are only a pathological gratification of the nerves and look about at the other tasteless graves everywhere, each grave is more tasteless than the next, Reger said. It is in the cemeteries that we see, quite brutally, the extreme tastelessness of humanity. Only grass grows on our grave and there is no name on our grave, Reger said, we agreed on that, my wife and I. No sentence, nothing. The stonemasons disfigure the cemeteries and the so-called sculptors put the crown of kitsch on them everywhere, Reger said. But you do get a marvelous view of Grinzing from my wife's grave, and of the Kahlenberg beyond. And of the Danube below. The grave is situated so high you can look down on Vienna from it. It certainly makes no difference where a person is buried, but if he happens to own a grave *for the lifetime of the cemetery*, as I and my wife do, then he should let himself be buried in his grave. I would rather be buried *anywhere except the Central Cemetery*, my wife often said, Reger said, and I myself would not like to be buried in the Central Cemetery either, even though, when all is said and done, it makes no difference where a person is buried. My nephew in Leoben, the only relative I still have, Reger said, knows that I do not wish to be buried in the Central Cemetery but *in my own grave, which is my property for the lifetime of the cemetery*, Reger said, but of course if I should die more than three hundred kilometres from Vienna, then *on the spot; within a three-hundred-kilometre radius of Vienna, otherwise on the spot*, I said to my Leoben nephew; he will stand by what I have told him because he is my heir, Reger said. Reger looked at the *White-Bearded Man* and said: only a year ago, shortly before my wife's death, I was quite fond of spending a couple of hours walking round Vienna, now I do not feel like it any longer. My wife's death has certainly weakened me a lot, I am not the man I was before her death. And besides, Vienna has become so ugly, he said. In winter I think spring will be my salvation, and in spring I think summer will be my salvation, and in summer I think autumn, and in autumn winter, it is always the same, I hope from one season to the next. But that of course is an unfortunate characteristic, this characteristic is congenital in me, I do not say, *how nice, it is now winter, winter is just what you need, any more than I say spring is just what you need, or autumn is just what you need, or summer and so on.* I keep blaming my misfortunes on the season I *have to* live in, *that* is my misfortune. I am not one of those people, who enjoy the present, that's what it is, I am one of those unfortunate ones who enjoy the past, that is the truth, those who always feel the present to be just an insult, that is the truth, Reger said, I feel the present to be an insult and an imposition, that is my misfortune. But of course it is not quite like that, Reger said, because time and again I am able to see the present as it is and, naturally, it is not always unhappy, or causing unhappiness, I know that, just as the past, if one thinks back to it, does not always make one happy, I know that. One great misfortune, of course, is the fact that I have no doctor in whom I have any confidence, I have had so many doctors in my life, but ultimately I had no confidence in any of those doctors, all of them ultimately let me down, Reger said. I feel utterly vulnerable and I feel that I might collapse at any moment. When I say, *strike me down*, I really believe that I might be struck down by a stroke, even though I have said those words a thousand times, Reger said, it even gets on my own nerves now, every other moment I say, *strike me down* but I have not been struck down, Reger said. In your presence, too, I have often said, *strike me down* but I have not been struck down, I do not say so just from habit but *because I really feel that I might be struck down*. As for my body, nothing is functioning properly any longer, Reger said. If only I had a good doctor, but I do not have a good doctor. Of course I have four general practitioners and two specialist physicians in the Singerstrasse, but none of these doctors is any good. My eyes are so bad I soon will not be able to see anything any more, but I have no good eye man. And of course I avoid seeing a doctor because I am afraid the doctor might *confirm what I suspect, that I am mortally ill.* I have been mortally ill for years, I always said so to my wife, Reger said, and I assumed as a matter of certainty that *I would die first, not she*, but then it was *she* who, because of all those frightful circumstances, died *before me* after all; I have had a great fear of doctors all my life. A good doctor is the best thing we can have, Reger said, but hardly anyone has a good doctor, we are forever dealing with medical bunglers and charlatans, he said, and if, exceptionally, we believe we find a good doctor, he is either too old or too young, he either knows something about the latest medicine and lacks experience or else he has experience and does not know anything about the latest medicine, that's how it is, Reger said. A person urgently needs a body healer and a soul healer and he does not find either, all his life he searches for a good body healer and a good soul healer and he finds neither, that is the truth. Do you know what the doctors at the Merciful Brethren said to me when I confronted them with the fact that they were responsible for my wife's death and therefore should have her on their conscience? They said, *her clock had run down*, they said this banal sentence to me and not just the one who bungled the operation on my wife said this sentence to me, all the doctors at the Merciful Brethren Hospital said this banal sentence, *her clock had run down, her clock had run down, her clock had run down*, they kept saying, as though this sentence were their standard sentence, Reger said. If we have a doctor in whom we can have confidence and under whose care we feel safe, Reger said, then we have the most important thing in old age, but we do not have such a doctor. I do not even look for such a doctor any longer because it is a matter of supreme, indifference to me when I die, any time would suit me, but like most people I want to have as quick and as painless a death as possible. My wife only suffered for a few days, Reger said, *suffered for a few days then for a few days in a coma*, he said. The people asked for a shroud but I had her wrapped simply in a clean sheet, Reger said. The man at the municipal office who handled the procedure of the funeral did his job quite superbly. It is a good idea to do everything connected with the funeral *ourselves*, then we do not have the time to sit at home and wait until we choke with despair. For eight days I chased about Vienna in connection with the funeral, one way and another, from one authority to another, and once again experienced the state in its entire bureaucratic brutality, Reger said. The authorities we have to seek out in Vienna in the event of a death are situated a long way away from one another and we need at least a whole week before we have completed all the business necessary for a funeral. Always and everywhere I said that I wanted *only the simplest funeral* for my wife, which they failed to understand, because everybody else, as I well know, always wants an extravagant one. The effort it cost me to *insist on the simplest funeral* in the end, Reger said. Only the man at the Währing municipal office understood me, he was the only one who understood that when I said *a simple funeral* I did not, as all the others believed, mean a cheap funeral but *simple one*, they all thought I wanted *a cheap one when I said a simple one*, only the man at the Währing municipal office instantly understood me when I said *a simple one, meaning a simple one and not a cheap one.* You would not believe how stupid the people whom you have to deal with at the authorities can be, Reger said. I did not think I would live to see this winter, let alone survive it, he now said. The fact is that I just existed throughout the past year with a total lack of interest in anything, apart from my concert engagements, and apart from my little works of art for *The Times* nothing in fact interested me any more after my wife's death; not a single person, that is the truth, including yourself, Reger said, for months I was not interested even in you. I read virtually nothing and did not leave the house except to go to concerts, but for this past year none of those concerts was worth going to and, naturally, my little works of art for *The Times were* accordingly. Sometimes I ask myself why I keep reporting *for The Times from Vienna*, seeing that in this confused Vienna things have gone into an alarming decline also in the musical sphere, because nothing out of the ordinary is being offered here in Vienna either at the Konzerthaus or at the Musikverein, Viennese concerts have long lost their unique quality, the same works which you hear in Vienna you could have heard much earlier in Hamburg or in Zurich or in Dinkelsbühl, Reger said. My eagerness to write is at its peak, but what Viennese concerts have to offer is worth less and less. I have long ceased to be the concert fanatic I once was, he said, *a music fanatic yes, but a concert fanatic no longer*, it is also getting more and more troublesome for me to go to the Musikverein or to the Konzerthaus, neither is easily accessible to me on foot and I do not take taxis and there is no tram there from the Singerstrasse. And the Konzerthaus audiences, just as the Musikverein audiences, have lately become very common and provincial, I have to say they are dulled and for years have no longer been knowledgeable, which is regrettable. The days when that singer of singers George London sang *Don Giovanni* at the Opera or the butcher's daughter Lipp the *Queen of the Night* are gone for good, as are the days when a sixty-year-old Menuhin conducted at the

Konzerthaus and a fifty-year-old Karajan at the Musik-verein. We now only hear the mediocre ones, the worthless ones. The idols, the top artists, the most ideal and the most competent performers have grown old and incompetent, Reger said. The present generation, curiously enough, no longer makes the highest demands on music, those which were made on music a mere fifteen or twenty years ago. The reason is that listening to music has become *a trivial everyday affair as a result of technical progress*. Listening to music is nothing out of the ordinary any more, you can hear music wherever you go, you are practically forced to hear music, in every department store, in every doctor's surgery, on every street, indeed you cannot *avoid* music nowadays, you wish to escape from it but you cannot escape, *this age is totally accompanied by background music*, that is the catastrophe, Reger said. Our age has witnessed the eruption of *total music*, anywhere between the North Pole and the South Pole you are forced to hear music, in the city or out in the country, on the high seas or in the desert, Reger said. People have been stuffed full of music every day for so long that they have long lost all feeling for music. This monstrous situation of course has its effect on the concerts you hear nowadays, there is nothing out of the ordinary nowadays because all music all over the world is out of the ordinary, and where everything is out of the ordinary there, naturally, nothing, out of the ordinary remains, indeed it is positively touching to see a few ridiculous virtuosi still taking pains to be out of the ordinary, but they are so no longer because they can be so no longer. The world is through and through *pervaded by total music*, Reger said, that is the misfortune, at every street corner you can hear extraordinary and perfect music on such a scale that you have probably blocked your ears long ago to stop yourself going out of your mind. People today, because they have nothing else left, suffer from a pathological music consumption, Reger said, this music consumption will be driven forward by the industry, which controls people today, to a point where everybody is destroyed; there is a lot of talk nowadays about waste and chemicals which have destroyed everything, but music destroys a lot more than waste and chemicals do, it is music that eventually will destroy absolutely everything *totally*, mark my words. The first thing to be destroyed by the music industry are people's auditory canals and next, as a logical consequence, the people themselves, that is the truth, Reger said. I can already see people totally destroyed by the music industry, Reger said, those masses of music-industry victims eventually populating the continents with their musical cadaverous stench, my dear Atzbacher, *the music industry will one day have the population on its conscience*, it will most probably ultimately have the whole of mankind on its conscience, not just chemicals and waste, believe me. The music industry is the murderer of human beings, the music industry is the real mass murderer of humanity which, if the music industry continues on its present lines, will have no hope whatever within a few decades, my dear Atzbacher, Reger said excitedly. A person with a sensitive ear will soon be unable to go out into the street; just go to a café, go to an inn, go to a department store, everywhere, whether you like it or not, you have to hear music; take a train or board a plane, music today pursues you everywhere. This ceaseless music is the most brutal thing present-day humanity has to suffer and to tolerate, Reger said. From early morning till late at night humanity is stuffed full of Mozart and Beethoven, Bach and Handel, Reger said. Go where you will, you cannot escape that torture. It is a downright miracle, Reger said, that ceaseless music is not yet to be heard at the Kunsthistorisches Museum as well, that would be the last straw. *After the funeral of my wife I locked myself up in the Singerstrasse flat and did not even admit the housekeeper*, Reger said. Immediately after the funeral he had gone to the nearby synagogue and lit a candle, without really knowing why, and the strangest thing was that from the synagogue he had gone straight into Saint Stephen's and lit a candle there too, again without really knowing why. Having lit a candle in Saint Stephen's, he had walked down the Wollzeile for some way with the idea of killing himself. However, I had no clear idea of *how* I would kill myself and eventually I was *able to dismiss* the idea of killing myself from my head, at least for a short time. I *had the choice between wandering criss-cross about the city for days and perhaps weeks, or staying locked up for weeks*, Reger said to me, I *decided in favour of staying locked up for weeks*. After his wife's funeral he had not wished to see anybody at all ever again and at first not even to eat anything ever again, but nobody could stand drinking nothing but pure water for days on end for more than three or four days, and he had in fact lost weight very rapidly and in the morning, suddenly, had *barely the strength to get up, that was a signal*, Reger said to me, and I started eating again and next I started studying Schopenhauer again, it was Schopenhauer my wife and I had been studying when she had her fall behind me and *broke the so-called neck of her femur*, Reger said thoughtfully. During these six weeks of locked-up existence I merely conducted a few telephone calls with my lawyer and read Schopenhauer, that probably saved me, Reger said, even though I am not sure whether it was right for me *to save* myself, probably, Reger said, it would have been better *not* to have saved myself, to have killed myself. But the mere fact that I had so much running about in connection with the funeral did not leave me any time to kill myself. Unless we kill ourselves *at once* we do not kill ourselves at all, that is what is so frightful, he said. We have the wish to be just as dead as the person we loved, but still we do not kill ourselves, we think about it but we do not do it, Reger said. Curiously enough I could not bear any music during those six weeks, I did not once sit down at the piano, *once in my mind I attempted a piece from the Well-Tempered Clavier, but immediately abandoned the attempt*, it was not music that was my salvation during those six weeks, *it was Schopenhauer, again and again a few lines of Schopenhauer*, Reger said. *It was not Nietzsche either, only Schopenhauer.* I sat up in bed and read a few lines of Schopenhauer and reflected on them and again read a few Schopenhauer sentences and reflected on them, Reger said. After four days of nothing but drinking water and reading Schopenhauer I ate my first piece of bread, which was so hard I had to chop it off the loaf with a meat cleaver. I sat down on the window stool facing the Singerstrasse, that hideous Loos stool, and looked down on the Singerstrasse. Imagine, it was the end of May and there was a flurry of snow. I shrank away from people. From my flat on the Singerstrasse I watched them rushing about down below, one way and another, laden with clothes and foodstuffs, and I felt nauseated by them. I thought I do not wish to go back among these people, *not among these people* and there are no others, Reger said. Looking down on to the Singerstrasse I realized that there were no other people than those rushing about the Singerstrasse this way and that. I looked down on to the Singerstrasse and hated the people and I said to myself I do not wish to go back among these people, Reger said. I do not wish to go back to that infamy and that shabbiness, I said to myself, Reger said. I pulled out several drawers and several chests and looked into them and kept taking out pictures and writings and correspondence of my wife and put everything on the table, one item after another, and progressively inspected everything, and because I am an honest person, my dear Atzbacher, I have to admit that I wept while doing so. Suddenly I gave my tears free rein, I had not wept for decades and suddenly I gave my tears free rein, Reger said. I sat there, giving my tears free rein, and I wept and wept and wept and wept, Reger said. I had not wept for decades, Reger said to me at the Ambassador. I have no need to conceal anything or to hide anything, he said, *with my eighty-two years I have no need to conceal or to hide anything at all*, Reger said, and I therefore do not conceal the fact that suddenly I wept and wept again, that I wept again for days, Reger said. I sat there, looking at the letters which my wife had written to me over the years and read the notes she had made over the years and just wept. Of course we get used to a person over the decades and love them for decades and eventually love them more than anything else and cling to them and when we lose them it is truly as if we had lost *everything.* I have always thought that it was music that meant everything to me, and at times that it was philosophy, or great or greatest or the very greatest writing, or altogether that it was simply art, but none of it, the whole of art or whatever, is nothing compared to that one beloved person. The things we inflicted on that one beloved person, Reger said, the thousands and hundreds of thousands of pains we inflicted on this one person whom we loved more than anyone else, the torments we inflicted on that person, and yet we loved them more than anyone else, Reger said. When that person whom we loved more than anyone else is dead they leave us with a terribly guilty conscience, Reger said, with a terribly guilty conscience with which we have to live after that person's death and which will choke us one day, Reger said. None of those books or writings which I had collected in the course of my life and which I had brought to the Singerstrasse flat to cram full all these shelves were ultimately any use, I had been left alone by my wife and all those books and writings were ridiculous. We think we can cling to Shakespeare or to Kant, but that is a fallacy, Shakespeare and Kant and all the rest, whom during our life we built up as the so-called great ones, let us down at the very moment when we would so badly need them, Reger said, they are no solution for us and they are no consolation to us, they suddenly seem revolting and alien to us, everything which those so-called great and important figures have thought and moreover written leaves us cold, Reger said. We always think we can rely on those so-called important and great ones, whichever, at the crucial moment, at the moment crucial in our lives, but that is a mistake, precisely at the moment which is crucial in our lives we find ourselves left alone by all those important and great ones, by those, as the saying goes, *immortal ones*, they provide us with no more at such a crucial moment in our lives than the fact that *even in their midst we are alone*, on our own in an utterly horrible sense, Reger said. Only and solely Schopenhauer helped me, *because quite simply I abused him for the purpose of my survival*, Reger said to me at the Ambassador. With all the others, including Goethe, Shakespeare and Kant, nauseating me I simply threw myself into Schopenhauer in my despair and sat down with Schopenhauer on my Singerstrasse-side stool in order to survive, for suddenly I wanted to survive and not to die, not to *follow* my wife but to remain *here*, to remain *in this world*, you understand, Atzbacher, Reger said at the Ambassador. But of course I had a chance of survival with Schopenhauer only because I abused him for my purposes *and in fact falsified him in the vilest manner*, Reger said, by quite simply turning him into a prescription for survival, which in fact he is not, any more than the others I have mentioned. All our lives we rely on the great minds and on the so-called old masters, Reger said, and then we are mortally disappointed by them because they do not fulfil their purpose at the crucial moment. We hoard the great minds and the old masters and we believe that at the crucial moment of survival we can use them for our purposes, which means nothing other than misusing them for our purposes, which turns out to be a fatal mistake. We fill our mental strong-room with these great minds and old masters and resort to them at the crucial moment in our lives; but when we unlock our mental strong-room it is empty, that is the truth, we stand before that empty mental strong-room and find that we are alone and in fact totally destitute, Reger said. A person hoards things all his life, in all fields, and in the end he stands there empty, Reger said, also where his mental possessions are concerned. Think of the colossal mental possessions I had hoarded, Reger said at the Ambassador, and in the end I am standing here totally empty. Only by dint of a vile trick did I succeed in misusing Schopenhauer for my purpose, for the purpose of my survival, Reger said. Suddenly you realize what emptiness is when you stand there amidst thousands and thousands of books and writings which have left you totally alone, which suddenly mean nothing to you except that terrible emptiness, Reger said. When you have lost your closest human being everything seems empty to you, look wherever you like, everything is empty, and you look and look and you see that everything is *really empty* and, what is more, for ever, Reger said. And you realize that it was not those great minds and not those old masters which kept you alive for decades but that it was this one single person whom you loved more than anyone else. And you stand alone in this realization and with this realization and there is nothing and no one to help you, Reger said. You lock yourself up in your flat in despair, Reger said, and from day to day your despair grows deeper and from week to week you get into ever more desperate despair, Reger said, yet suddenly you emerge from that despair. You get up and walk out of that mortal despair, you still have the strength to walk out of that deepest despair, Reger said, suddenly I got up from the Singerstrasse-side stool and walked out of my despair and down into the Singerstrasse, Reger said,

and walked a few hundred yards into the Inner City;
I got up from the Singerstrasse-side stool and walked
out of my flat and into the Inner City with the idea
of making just one single attempt, an attempt at
survival, Reger said. I walked out of the Singerstrasse
flat and I thought I will make one more, one single,
attempt at survival and with this idea I walked into the
Inner City, Reger said. And this attempt at survival was
successful, I probably got up from the Singerstrasse-
side stool at the crucial and probably the very last
moment to walk down into the Singerstrasse and into
the Inner City, Reger said. Naturally, back home in
my flat I experienced one relapse after another, *you
will realize that this one single attempt at survival was
not enough, I had to make several hundred such survival
attempts*, but I did make them, time and again, and I
would get up, time and again, from my Singerstrasse-
side stool and walk out into the street and actually
back among people, among *those* people, and eventually
saved myself, Reger said. Of course I ask myself
whether it was right and not, after all, a mistake to
save myself, but that is not the point, Reger said. We
sincerely wish to *follow* someone into death and yet
we do not then wish to go through with it, Reger said,
that is the torment of despair in which I have existed,
if you know what I mean, for over a year now. We
hate people and yet we want to be with them because

only with people and among people do we stand a chance of carrying on without going insane. We cannot in fact bear to be alone for very long, Reger said, we believe we can be alone, we believe we can be left on our own, we persuade ourselves that we can manage on our own, Reger said, but this is a chimera. Without people we have not the slightest hope of survival, Reger said, no matter how many great minds and old masters we have taken on as companions, *they do not replace a human being*, Reger said, *in the end we are abandoned by all those so-called great minds and by all those so-called old masters and we realize that we are, on top of it, being mocked in the vilest manner by these great minds and old masters* and we find that with all those great minds and with all those old masters we have always only had a mocking relationship. To begin with, he said, he had only lived on bread and water at the Singerstrasse flat, later, on about the eighth or ninth day, he had eaten a little tinned meat, which he had himself heated up in the kitchen, he had soaked some dried prunes and eaten them with noodles over which he had poured boiling water, after which however he had felt sick each time. On the eighth or ninth day eventually he had ordered his housekeeper to return and had sent her across the road to the Hotel Royal to bring him back a meal. He had come to a convenient arrangement with the Hotel Royal, *from*

*the end of May onward they have supplied me every day,
by way of the housekeeper whom we had always called
Stella although her name was Rosa*, Reger said, *with
soup and a main course in aluminium containers specially
bought for the purpose. I pay for two helpings*, Reger said
to me at the Ambassador, I *would eat half a helping and
the housekeeper a helping and a half*, Reger said. I ate the
Royal food with a certain reluctance, Reger said, but
I ate it because I had no choice, I ate it because I had
to eat it, Reger said, but then I would feel sick just at
the sight of the housekeeper who, naturally, sat
facing me during the meal, I could never stand the
housekeeper, but then she was my wife's housekeeper,
I myself would have never engaged that person,
Reger said, that stupid, lying person, Reger said, who
actually sat facing me, eating one and a half helpings
of the Royal food while I only ate half a one. We
accept housekeepers because otherwise we would
choke in our dirt, Reger said at the Ambassador, but
all in all they are always distasteful. We are dependent
on housekeepers, that's what it is, Reger said. Besides,
she would always bring over from the Royal the dishes
she wanted to eat, the ones she had chosen *for herself*,
and not the dishes which I would have liked. She
preferred pork, so she always brought over pork, but
I only eat beef if I am asked, Reger said, I have always
been a beef eater, housekeepers are all pork eaters.

After my wife's death, in fact immediately after the funeral, Reger said, the housekeeper drew my attention to the fact that my wife had *bequeathed* her this and that, Reger said, although I know that my wife never bequeathed anything to the housekeeper, since my wife never thought about dying and never spoke *to anybody about things to be bequeathed or to be left*, not even to me, let alone to the housekeeper. But the house-keeper came to me immediately after the funeral and told me my wife had left this and that to her, clothes, shoes, pots and pans, materials, and so on. Housekeepers never flinch from any embarrass-ment, Reger said at the Ambassador. They are utterly shameless in their demands. Everyone everywhere sings the praises of housekeepers, even though people know perfectly well that today's housekeepers do not deserve praise, today's housekeepers are distasteful in their demands and utterly slovenly in their work, but people are hypocrites and say that housekeepers deserve praise because they are dependent on them, Reger said at the Ambassador. My wife never even for an instant thought of leaving the housekeeper anything, even two days before her death my wife did not suspect that she would die, so how could she have promised anything to the housekeeper? Reger asked. She is lying, I thought, when the housekeeper drew my attention to the fact that my wife had promised her various articles, the funeral guests had not even left the cemetery when the housekeeper appeared before me to say that my wife had promised her this and that. Time and again we stand up for people because we cannot believe and do not want to believe that they can be so vile, until, over and over again, we discover that they are far more vile than we would credit. Several times, when I was still standing by the open grave, the housekeeper said the words *frying pan*, Reger said, imagine it, again and again the words *frying pan* while I was still standing by the open grave. For weeks the housekeeper kept pestering me with the infamous lie that my wife had promised her *a lot*. However, as the saying goes, I *turned a deaf ear*. Not until three months after my wife's death did I tell the housekeeper she should *choose some* of the clothes, which I had intended for my wife's nieces, and take whatever pots and pans she found useful. You cannot imagine how the housekeeper acted in response to this! Reger said, the person snatched whole armfuls of clothes to herself and stuffed them into large two-hundred-pound bags which she had all ready, until nothing more would go into those bags. I stood there, flabbergasted, watching the scene. Like a lunatic the housekeeper ran through the flat, grabbing up whatever she could grab up. In the end she had filled five two-hundred-pound bags and crammed whatever

would not go into the two-hundred-pound bags,
into three large cases. Eventually her daughter also
appeared on the scene, and the two jointly lugged
down the bags and the cases into the Singerstrasse,
where the daughter had parked a borrowed van. When
the two had carried all the bags and cases down to the
Singerstrasse the housekeeper in addition ranged
dozens of casseroles on the floor, without even asking
if I minded her taking those casseroles as well. After
all, she was *letting me keep* this casserole or that, she
said, while tying up the casseroles with string threaded
through the casserole handles in order to carry them
down more easily to the Singerstrasse. I stood
there, flabbergasted, watching the housekeeper and
her daughter as, like lunatics, they dragged these
casseroles down out of the flat as well. My wife had
never even seen the housekeeper's daughter, Reger
said, if she had seen her once at least in the many years
the housekeeper was in service with us, she would
have been aghast at the sight, Reger said. The more
we invest in a person, in a manner of speaking, and
the kinder we are to them, the worse they repay us,
Reger said at the Ambassador. This experience with
the housekeeper and her daughter once again demonstrated to me how abysmally hideous man can be,
Reger said. The so-called lower orders, surely this
is the truth, are every bit as vile and infamous and

every bit as mendacious as the upper classes. This is actually one of the most repulsive characteristics of our age that it is always claimed that the so-called simple and the so-called oppressed people are good and the others bad, that is one of the most repulsive lies I know, Reger said. The so-called housekeeper is no better than the so-called mistress, and anyway things are really the other way round nowadays, as indeed everything nowadays is the other way round, Reger said, surely the housekeeper is the mistress nowadays, not the other way round. The so-called powerless are the powerful today, not the other way round, Reger said at the Ambassador. While he was now gazing at the *White-Bearded Man* I could still hear what he had said to me at the Ambassador, that everything today was the other way round, over and over again that *everything today is the other way round*. I was still standing by the open grave when the housekeeper buttonholed me, asserting that my wife had bequeathed her the green winter coat she had bought in Badgastein. That beautiful expensive coat, of all things, the idea that my wife would have bequeathed that to the housekeeper, Reger said angrily. These people exploit any situation and shrink from nothing, stupid though they are, these people turn anything, even the most distasteful things, to their advantage. And we fall for these people time and again, because in the distastefulness of everyday matters they are of course superior to us, Reger said. That hypocrisy about the people is another repulsive thing, those pledges to the people which are so typical of, for instance, our politicians. Whenever we have an idealistic notion it always turns out very soon that this notion is nothing but a nonsensical notion, Reger said; we all have to grow old, and there is nothing more repulsive than this currying of favour with the young, this has always profoundly repelled me, when an old person tries to curry favour with the young, my dear Atzbacher, and he said a person today is at everyone's mercy, unprotected, we are dealing today with a totally un-protected person, totally at everyone's mercy, a mere decade ago people still felt more or less protected but today they are exposed to total unprotectedness, Reger said at the Ambassador. They can no longer hide, there is no hiding place left, that is what is so terrible, Reger said, everything has become transparent and thereby unprotected; in other words there is no hope of escape left today, people, no matter where they are, are everywhere hustled and incited and flee and escape and no longer find a refuge to escape to, unless of course they choose death, that is a fact, Reger said, that is the sinister aspect, because the world today is no longer mysterious but only sinister. With this sinister world you have to come to terms, Atzbacher, whether you like it or not, *you are completely and totally at the mercy of this sinister world* and if someone tries to tell you otherwise then he is trying to tell you a lie, today's lie which is ceaselessly drummed into your ears, the lie on which the politicians and the political twaddlers have specialized, Reger said. The world is one big sinister place where no one can find shelter any more, no one, Reger said at the Ambassador. Reger was looking at the *White-Bearded Man* and said, the death of my wife has not only been my greatest misfortune, it has also set me free. With the death of my wife I have become free, he said, and when I say *free* I mean *entirely free, wholly free, completely free*, if you know, or if at least you surmise, what I mean. I am no longer waiting for death, it will come by itself, it will come without my thinking of it, it does not matter to me when. The death of a beloved person is also an enormous liberation of our whole system, Reger now said. I have lived for some time now with the feeling of being totally free. I *can now let anything approach me, really anything, without having to resist, I no longer resist anything, that is it*, Reger now said. Looking at the *White-Bearded Man* he said, I have always really loved the *White-Bearded Man*. I never loved Tintoretto, but I have loved Tintoretto's *White-Bearded Man*. I have looked at this painting for over thirty years and I still find it possible to look at it, there is no other painting I could have looked at for over thirty years. The old masters tire quickly if we study them scrupulously and they always disappoint us if we subject them to closer scrutiny, if, as it were, we make them the ruthless object of our critical intellect. Not one of these so-called old masters will stand up to such a truly critical scrutiny, Reger now said. Leonardo, Michelangelo, Titian, all this dissolves in our eyes with incredible rapidity and ultimately reveals itself as paltry survival art, no matter how inspired, as a paltry attempt at survival. Now Goya is a tougher nut, Reger said, but even Goya ultimately is no use to us and means nothing to us. Everything here at the Kunsthistorisches Museum, which incidentally does not even possess a Goya, Reger now said, ultimately means nothing to us, I *mean at the crucial point in our existence*, nothing at all. In all these pictures, if we study them intensively, we sooner or later discover an awkwardness, or indeed, even in the very greatest and the most important creations, a flaw, if we are uncompromising, *a serious flaw* which gradually makes us dislike these pictures, probably because we pitched our expectations too high, Reger said. Art altogether is nothing but a survival skill, we should never lose sight of this fact, it is, time and again, just an attempt – an attempt that seems touching even to our intellect – to cope with this world and its revolting aspects, which, as we know, is invariably possible only by resorting to lies and falsehoods, to hypocrisy and self-deception, Reger said. These pictures are full of lies and falsehoods and full of hypocrisy and self-deception, there is nothing else in them if we disregard their often inspired artistry. All these pictures, moreover, are an expression of man's absolute helplessness in coping with himself and with what surrounds him all his life. That is what all these pictures express, this helplessness which, on the one hand, embarrasses the intellect and, on the other, bewilders the same intellect and moves it to tears, Reger said. The *White-Bearded Man* has stood up to my intellect and to my feelings for over thirty years, Reger said, to me it is therefore the most precious item on show here at the Kunsthistorisches Museum. As though I had realized this over thirty years ago, I sat down on this settee here for the first time over thirty years ago, *directly facing the White-Bearded Man. All these so-called old masters are really failures, without exception they were all doomed to failure, and the viewer can establish this failure in every detail of their works, in every brush-stroke*, Reger said, *in the smallest and very smallest detail*. Quite apart from the fact that of all these so-called old masters each one invariably only painted some detail of his pictures with real genius, not one of them painted a one-hundred-per-cent picture of genius, not one of those so-called old masters ever succeeded in doing that; either they failed with the chin or with the knee or with the eyelids, Reger said. Most of them failed with the hands, there is not a single painting to be seen in the Kunsthistorisches Museum on which there is a hand painted with genius, or even painted with extraordinary competence, always only those tragicomically unsuccessful hands, Reger said, that is what you see here in all these portraits, even the most celebrated ones. Nor did any of these so-called old masters succeed in painting even an exceptional chin or a truly successful knee. El Greco never managed to paint even a single hand, El Greco's hands all look like dirty wet face flannels, Reger now said, but then there is not a single El Greco in the Kunsthistorisches Museum anyway. And Goya, who is likewise not represented in the Kunsthistorisches Museum, carefully avoided painting even a single hand *clearly*, where Goya's hands are concerned even Goya got stuck in dilettantism, this terrifying monstrous Goya, whom I place above all painters who ever painted, Reger said. Besides, it is downright depressing, here in this Kunsthistorisches Museum, only ever to see an art which should be labelled state art, an anti-spiritual Habsburg-Catholic state art. It has been the same for decades, I come to the Kunsthistorisches Museum and think that the Kunsthistorisches Museum does not even have a Goya! That it does not have an El Greco is not, as far as I and my view of art are concerned, a tragedy, but that the Kunsthistorisches Museum should not have a Goya is truly a tragedy, Reger said. If we apply an international yardstick, Reger said, then we must admit that the Kunsthistorisches Museum, contrary to its reputation, is not really a first-class museum because it does not even have the great all-outclassing Goya. On top of this is the fact that the Kunsthistorisches Museum is entirely in line with the artistic taste of the Habsburgs, who, at least where painting is concerned, had a revolting, totally brainless Catholic artistic taste. The Catholic Habsburgs never cared much more for painting than they did for literature, because painting and literature always *seemed to them dangerous arts, unlike music*, which could never become dangerous to them and which the Catholic Habsburgs, just because they were so brainless, *allowed to unfold to full flower*, as I once read in a so-called *art book*. Habsburg falseness, Habsburg feeble-mindedness, Habsburg perversity in matters of faith, these are what you see hanging on all these walls, that is the truth, Reger said. And in all these pictures, even in the landscapes, that perverse Catholic infantilism in matters of faith. Vulgar ecclesiastical hypocrisy even in the paintings with the highest, the very highest, claim to pictorial perfection, that is what is so repulsive. Everything exhibited at the Kunsthistorisches Museum wears a Catholic halo, not even excepting Giotto, Reger said. These repulsive Venetians who, with every paw they ever painted, cling to the Catholic pre-Alp heaven, he now said. You cannot find *a single natural painted face* in the Kunsthistorisches Museum, *always only a Catholic visage.* Just look at any well-painted head here for some length of time, in the end it will be just a Catholic head, Reger said. Even the grass in these paintings grows as Catholic grass and the soup in the Dutch soup bowls is nothing but Catholic soup, Reger now said. Shameless painted Catholicism, that is what it is, Reger said. The reason why I have been coming to the Kunsthistorisches Museum these thirty-six years was only that an ideal temperature of eighteen degrees Celsius is maintained here all the year round, the best temperature not only for the canvas of these works of art but also for my skin and above all for my highly sensitive head, Reger said. *Intensive study of art, suicidal method, achieved a certain senior-league championship,* Reger now said. *No customary law at the Kunsthistorisches Museum,* he said, *hatred of art basically, incurable art madness.* Undoubtedly, my dear Atzbacher, we have nearly reached the peak of our age of chaos and kitsch, he said, adding: the whole of this Austria, when all is said and done, is nothing but a Kunsthistorisches

Museum, a Catholic-National-Socialist one, an appalling one. *Hypocritical display of democracy*, he said. A chaotic rubbish-heap, that is what today's Austria is, this ridiculous pygmy state which drips with self-overestimation and which, forty years after the so-called *Second World War*, has reached its absolute low only as a totally amputated state; this ridiculous pygmy state, where thought has died out and where for half a century now only base state-political dull-wittedness and state-adoring stupidity have reigned, Reger said. A confused brutal world, he said. Too old to disappear, he said, I am too old to make my exit, Atzbacher, eighty-two, you know! Always been alone! Now I am finally trapped, Atzbacher. Wherever we look in this country today, we look into a cesspit of ludicrousness, Reger said. Disastrous mass madness, he said. Everyone is more or less depressive, you know, and we share with Hungary the highest suicide rate in the whole of Europe. I have often thought I would go to Switzerland, but Switzerland would be a lot worse for me still. You have no idea *how* I love this country, Reger said, but I most profoundly hate this present state; I do not wish to have anything to do with *this* state in future, it gets more nauseating every day. All those acting and ruling in this state have nothing but horrible primitively brainless faces, all you see in this bankrupt country now is a gigantic heap of alarming physiognomic refuse, he said. The things we think and the things we say, believing that we are competent and yet we are not, *that is the comedy*, and when we ask *how is it all to continue? that is the tragedy*, my dear Atzbacher. Irrsigler appeared with *The Times* which Reger had asked him to get for him, he only had to cross the road from the Kunsthistorisches Museum to the newspaper stand opposite. Reger took *The Times* and got up and walked out of the Bordone Room and, as it seemed to me, with a brisker step, down the great central staircase and into the open, and I followed him. He stopped at the vulgar Maria Theresa Monument and said that I was probably rather astonished that he had still not told me the *real* reason *why* he had wished to meet me at the Kunsthistorisches Museum *again today*. I scarcely believed my ears when he said he had bought *two tickets, excellent seats in the stalls, for the Broken Pitcher at the Burgtheater* and the *real* reason why he had asked me to the Kunsthistorisches Museum again today was to invite me to see the *Broken Pitcher* at the Burgtheater with him. You realize that I have not been to the Burgtheater for decades and that I hate nothing more than the Burgtheater, *in fact nothing more than dramatic art generally*, he said, but I thought yesterday I will go to the Burgtheater tomorrow and see the *Broken Pitcher*. My dear Atzbacher, Reger said, I do not know what gave me the idea of going to the Burgtheater today and more particularly with you and with no other person in order to see the *Broken Pitcher*. I do not mind if you think me crazy, Reger now said, my days are numbered anyway; I really thought you might go to the Burgtheater with me today, the *Broken Pitcher*, after all, is the best German comedy and the Burgtheater moreover is the foremost stage in the world. For three hours I was tormented by the thought that I would have to ask you to accompany me to the *Broken Pitcher*, because I will not see the *Broken Pitcher* on my own, Reger now said, Atzbacher records, for three tormenting hours I reflected how I could tell you that I have bought two tickets for the *Broken Pitcher* and in doing so thought *only of myself and you*, because for decades you have been hearing from me nothing but that the Burgtheater is the most hideous theatre in the world and now, all of a sudden, you are to go with me to see the *Broken Pitcher* at the Burgtheater, a fact which even Irrsigler cannot understand. *Take the second ticket*, he said, *and come with me to the Burgtheater this evening, share my enjoyment of this perverse folly, my dear Atzbacher*, Reger said, Atzbacher records. Very well, I said to Reger, Atzbacher records, *if that is your express wish*, and Reger said, *yes, it is my express wish* and handed me the second ticket. I actually went with Reger to the Burgtheater in the evening to see the *Broken Pitcher*, Atzbacher records. The performance was terrible.